This book is a work of fiction. Names, characters, places, events, and other factors are the fruit of the author's imagination or have been used fictitiously and are not to be construed as real. All the characters in the book remain fictitious and any resemblance to persons, living or dead, actual events, locales, or organizations is entirely coincidental.

Traveller, mystery novel enthusiast,
this story is for you.
As ever, Gwyneth

DEDICATION

I dedicate this book to those members of my family who supported me during this adventure. In particular I would like to mention my two daughters: Véronique for her excellent close readings of the text as well as her interesting suggestions; Joanna for tirelessly undertaking and carrying out all the preparation necessary to present it for publication and the publishing itself.

Love, Gwyneth

TABLE OF CONTENTS

1	Dog Days	Pg 1
2	Paris Story	Pg 15
3	Casque d'Or	Pg 31
4	Home Run	Pg 47
5	The Montreal Connection	Pg 63
6	The Long Arm	Pg 79
7	Moles Galore	Pg 93
8	What Are Friends For?	Pg 107
9	The Information Highway	Pg 121
10	Atishoo, We All Fall Down	Pg 135
11	It's a Cat's Life	Pg 141
12	The Ravel'd Sleeve	Pg 157
13	Still Waters	Pg 171
14	Knitting Patterns	Pg 187
15	The Gift Horse	Pg 201
16	Let There Be Light	Pg 217
17	Epilogue	Pg 229

"...a delightful read! Ms. Williams' knowledge of both Montreal and Paris provides a picturesque background as she weaves her story in and out, dropping tantalizing clues as weft through the warp. Those who are devotees of the Oxford English Dictionary will appreciate her use of marvelous descriptors. We look forward to the continuing adventures of the intrepid Sara." Dr. Jane, psychologist

ACKNOWLEDGMENTS

To all family, friends and unknowing authors who have unwittingly contributed so much to my book! Thank you,

Yours in harmony, Gwyneth

Gwyneth Williams Mystery

LAST STEP

How does a seemingly nice middle-class middle-aged professional woman come to be involved in murder in one country only to have it follow her back to another country? Why does her eclectic mix of acquaintances and interests intrigue the police of these two nations so much? What is it about their mother that, when called upon, her daughters are so willing to bend the rules? Can friends be trusted? An intercontinental intrigue that will have you laughing, sighing and surprised by the end of it.

"Her family would surely be very proud of her for pulling off such a good translation contract in France. And she could enjoy the rest of her rather brief holiday in Paris."

"The publishing firm had even agreed to cover the cost of her Montreal-Paris return flight."

"Was wasting money worse or better than murder, Sara wondered, but decided to keep her question to herself."

"She went on to read that, while several other avenues were being explored, the Paris police were concentrating their efforts on the victim's trip to Montreal."

CHAPTER ONE

Dog Days

Sara, as bemused as the fictional Lord Littlemore's guests appeared to be, slammed the book shut. Was this really the book she had agreed to translate? Could this really be the fruit of all her efforts to find a French publisher languishing for want of a good translator? Had she signed too quickly and without paying enough attention…?

"Thank you all for attending this little gathering." Lord Littlemore was at his most suave, as he waved rather a languid hand around the library to include all the guests in his greeting. Ten people were gathered before him, all but one perched on antique ladder-back chairs or ensconced in the few leather armchairs scattered here and there. The exception, the butler, stood impassively by the door, almost as if he were guarding it, although his stance -- that of the perfect manservant, arms straight down at his side, hands turned slightly outwards -- was in no way threatening. The atmosphere in the room was one of puzzlement. Why indeed had Lord Littlemore invited them all there? And why was he receiving them in the library rather than in the sitting room? It was an odd arrangement.

But their host had already launched into an explanation. "Tony's and Angela's murderer is among us," he said. "I have brought you all here tonight," he bowed, as if to acknowledge their graciousness in bending to his will, "in order to unmask the villain. Your drinks have been served; there are snacks on all the tables. There is no reason for you to be uncomfortable, except for the murderer," here he smiled sardonically, "while I a tale unfold, of love, hate and greed. A tale that culminates in murder and revenge." An incredulous murmur filled the room.

It was hard to believe they were actually going to pay her for translating such a bunch of nonsense. And not just one book either. A whole series. She'd forgotten how many. Each one probably worse than the one before. It was an author she'd never even heard of, let alone read. Straight out of the: "Anyone for tennis school" by the look of things. Yes, the original copyright was 1933. Although some of those earlier mystery novels had been absolutely brilliant.

How odd of the French to want to read something so clearly out-of-date. Ah well, it probably suited them to think of England as permanently locked into some kind of *Private Lives* type scenario. They seemed to like their Americans to be violent and their Brits to be willowy. Rambo versus the Scarlet Pimpernel. All very different from the French heroes of the same period, the most endearing among them being the famous *Inspecteur Maigret*, no doubt, although his creator, Georges Simenon, was as Belgian as the fictitious *Hercule Poirot* thought up by Agatha C. Certainly none of the major writers had produced many women detectives until fairly recently. Still, if she didn't lose her mind in the process, she'd be in clover for some time to come. The terms she'd just negotiated were very favourable, among the best she'd ever had, and the publishing firm had even agreed to cover the cost of her Montreal-Paris return flight.

Her family would surely be very proud of her for pulling off such a good translation contract in France. And she could enjoy the rest of her rather brief holiday in Paris without feeling guilty about the money she was spending. Buy yet another pair of shoes perhaps. Although getting them past Customs was always a problem since the increases in travellers' allowances rarely kept pace with the inflation in prices. Sara decided to sleep on that and spend the rest of the afternoon at the *Institut du monde arabe*, which she hadn't revisited since its early days. They seemed always to organize such splendid exhibitions that she could rarely see because of the distance. A bridge over the Atlantic sounded like a great solution!

A cursory glance at her bus and metro plan confirmed that a bus she often had occasion to take for different errands would take her to a point only a few streets away from her destination. Such bliss to be in a city with so many fascinating museums and art galleries. Such bliss also to be in a city where walking is a pleasure. All sorts of little streets and hidden alleyways often filled with treasures and the 5th arrondissement located on the Left Bank of the river Seine was simply delightful.

She paid her bill in the little *café* where she'd stopped to have a celebratory *pastis*, with its delicate licorice flavor, and a little snack, hesitating as usual about whether to leave a tip on the tip. It seemed called for now even though the service was included in the price. Eventually she decided, again and as usual, against it. Apparently women were considered bad tippers, but Sara knew that they often didn't get such good service as men and believed they were quite right to tip accordingly. Once in Montreal, the group of women she was with had collectively refused to leave any tip at all. What a row that had led to!

She added the book she'd been glancing at to the pile in her briefcase and, dodging a variety of cars, trucks, motorbikes, scooters and a number of other hazards, made it across the street to the bus stop. At that very moment, miracles do happen, the one she wanted pulled up.

Proudly, she flashed her bus pass. Just having one gave her the illusion of really living permanently in Paris. Then she lurched to a seat at the back of the bus as the urban cowboy at the wheel swung round a few corners as if he were practicing to be Alain Prost or some other Formula I racing champion. Having made it without damage to life or limb, she first gave praise to the goddess, then settled in to look at her fellow travellers, as no doubt some of them were

LAST STEP

looking at her. What did they see? Sara hoped she did not look old enough yet to be called elderly and opted for being described as a breathless middle-aged woman carrying a brief-case as well as a purse and wearing a rather elegant -- again she hoped -- cotton dress and the smart shoes with heels, albeit low, that are de rigueur in the French capital? A male -- chauvinist -- acquaintance had once told her that you could tell a woman's age by the height of her heels, she remembered; in Paris you could certainly usually tell the tourists from the natives by the smartness of their footwear.

Alas, the other passengers looked to her like rather a dull lot, on the whole. No stories to make up there. Even the colourful costumes worn by so many apparently immigrant women, possibly African or Pakistani, she said to herself, costumes that leavened the more traditional French garb, couldn't make their owners appear anything but respectable, conservative even. Unusually enough, the bus wasn't crowded. Perhaps all those who had travelled on it during the long and boring ride from its starting point in an unendearing northern suburb had decided for once to get off *en masse* at the *Gare de l'Est*, a beautifully restored railway station that mainly served France's eastern neighbours, as its name would suggest. They might be heading away to Strasbourg or Munich or other more exotic destinations. Perhaps aboard the Orient Express even. Ah, Agatha Christie, Ngaio Marsh, Margery Allingham, and all your colleagues, where are you now?

The most interesting looking person was already well settled in only a few centimetres away from her, almost at right angles on the long curved bench seat. A rabbi, she decided, without really knowing anything about it. Certainly an Orthodox person of some kind. A Hassidic Jew perhaps? Apart from what appeared to be a little ringlet escaping from beneath the large-brimmed hat he was wearing, he had the soft peachy skin of someone who'd never shaved; perhaps that was why he looked so young. At least his neck and ears did. She couldn't see his face, and that wasn't surprising if what she'd read about Hassidic customs was correct. They weren't allowed to raise their eyes to look at other people, she believed, rather like delicately nurtured maidens of previous centuries. This one was also fast asleep, his head, bent forward, lolling gently from side to side with the movement of the bus. Another good reason why his face would remain invisible. She felt quite motherly towards him; sitting there, pale and limp, he really did look dreadfully young and vulnerable, as young boys do when they still have down upon their cheeks.

The clear plastic bag on his lap looked inviting. She cast a semi-professional glance at its contents; old books, indeed all books, were always of interest to her. These, about a dozen in all, were all leather bound. Some were crumbling a little around the edges with age, but all were *dorés sur tranche* as the French might say, luxurious with gilt lettering on their spines. The language must surely have been Hebrew; certainly it was nothing she could understand. Odd that he should carry probably expensive, even unique, volumes in a plastic bag and so risk damaging them in the process. No doubt he had some valid reason for it, if only poverty.

She opened her own briefcase at that point and pulled

out yet another paperback thriller, one she was reading for her own pleasure and hadn't quite finished. There were another couple of short chapters to go, although she already had a fairly good idea both of the identity of the murderer and the motive for the crime. The cover was really rather lurid; one could only keep one's fingers crossed that the young rabbi, if he was indeed a rabbi, would not be shocked should his wakening gaze fall upon it. He certainly wasn't likely ever actually to read anything so worldly.

Hoping the last pages would prove her judgment right, she opened the book where she had left off and, absorbed in her reading, forgot to look out the window at her surroundings. She remained oblivious to the crowded streets going by, eager shoppers going from stall to stall, cheapjacks crying their wares, pedestrians crossing from one side of the road to the other at risk of life and limb, idlers simply chatting in the sun.

Even the summer heat seemed to weigh less on her as her eyes avidly skimmed the print, looking for confirmation of her guesses. Ah! Another murder, one she hadn't expected, but it hardly changed the main plot. Once again, she'd followed every clue to its logical conclusion, thus doubling the pleasure she always derived from a good mystery. A little self-satisfaction is a wonderful thing! she thought as she closed her book. Particularly when it's justified.

As she put it away in her briefcase, she cast a wondering glance at her neighbour on the seat, admiring his ability to sleep his way through the journey. It was almost unnatural. Besides he might miss, might already have missed, his stop. They were well into, in fact almost leaving by now, that beautiful old area of Paris, le Marais, where there were quite a few synagogues. Still, one mustn't assume that was where he was heading. Watch your stereotypes... Nevertheless, even if he had quite a different destination, the terminus would be upon them as soon as they crossed the river and then he'd have to get off.

To wake or not to wake, and, in particular, to wake or not to wake someone who probably wasn't allowed contact with others. A Hamlet-type dilemma. Would he have to expiate in some way afterwards, if she went ahead and woke him, or was expiation a particularly Christian concept? She would ask someone someday.

For now, what happened to him wasn't necessarily any of her business, indeed, it clearly was the opposite of her business, but turning her back on others was something she had found difficult since childhood. Still, it was rather daunting to think he might cower back in horror if she so much as touched him. Or was that exaggerating what might happen? Ah well, time to act.

But, as in the best detective novels, fate intervened. Confronted for once by a fairly clear one-way stretch of road, the bus driver had picked up speed, at the very moment that a parked sports car, oblivious to anything but its own interests, pulled sharply away from the sidewalk. The bus driver, cursing rather imaginatively, wrenched the steering wheel from left to right while jamming on his brakes in order to avoid a crash. The sleeping rabbi, caught in the countermotion, first sat bolt upright then shot forward to land face downward on Sara's lap. From whence he didn't move.

Sara looked down to remonstrate. Any statement she intended to make remained stillborn. Protruding from the back of the burden she now carried on her knees was something small and shiny, something that, however little, was clearly the hilt of a knife. Shrieking in shock and horror, she leapt to her feet, and the body slumped clumsily to the floor of the bus.

"*Arrêtez, Arrêtez!*" she cried. "*Il ne faut plus partir!* Stop the bus! There's a dead man on the back seat!" Most of the other passengers immediately assumed that abstracted expression that indicated they recognized a crazy woman when they saw one and had no intention of becoming further involved. A few rushed toward her, probably, she thought afterwards, with a view to pinioning her arms and turning her over to the nearest authorities. They might even murmur virtuously: "good riddance!"

They stopped short, however, when they saw the corpse and immediately began a frenzied discussion about what to do next. "Pick him up," said one. "Certainly not," said another, "we must leave him where he is." "Call the Samu," added a third. "Their job is to deal with medical emergencies." "What medical emergency," responded the first. "This man doesn't need treatment. He's dead. He's not just dead, either. He's been murdered."

"Murdered!" The word travelled round the bus, and, in the hubbub, more and more passengers got up to see what was happening. One of them even pulled out a camera and started frenziedly clicking away at anything and everybody. For all the world like the Japanese tourist of popular imagination or some Italian paparazzo of the same ilk, Sara was to say later, when she was describing the scene to her daughters. Cell phones appeared and the images would certainly find their way online in the near future. She, in the meantime, was still trying to find a place to stand or sit where her feet would not be encumbered by the corpse of her former neighbour. She was also anxious not to give the impression she was trying to escape.

At that point, the bus driver, a stocky, rather self-important looking man with an incipient beard, intervened. Shouldering his way to the back, he indicated in no uncertain terms that he wanted no confusion and disorder in any vehicle under his command. He was clearly still under the impression that he was dealing with either an hysterical female or some kind of film crew that hadn't consulted him before organizing its shenanigans. When he reached the little group, huddling around Sara and still arguing about what best to do with the grisly object before them, he was forced to stand on tiptoe to discover exactly what was creating all the disturbance. At first, unable to see anything, he started ordering people to stand back but suddenly, in a gap, his eye fell upon the body and the knife sticking out of it. He blanched.

For a few seconds, he couldn't react. He stood stock still, like one turned to stone. Then suddenly, grumbling and muttering to himself: "*Pas vrai, il n'y a qu'à moi, ma dernière course de la journée*, the inspector's going to have fits over the delay, I'll never get off work and there'll be no overtime for this, I'm going to miss the game on TV, what have I done *au bon Dieu* to deserve it?". He spun on his heels and rushed to his seat in order to radio a message back to his control centre and ask for instructions.

Quite a few passengers now turned on him, demanding to be let off. Trying to explain the situation to a disbelieving inspector and simultaneously understand his response over a radio crackling with static, he waved them to silence. Unfortunately his gestures inflamed rather than appeased them. They all proffered excellent reasons for leaving the stinking bus: urgent appointments with doctors, dentists, radiologists, lawyers; none of them seemed merely to be going home or be on their way to visit friends or do a little shopping. Amazing.

The bus driver was adamant, however, in spite of one man's threats to bring the affair before the highest powers in the land. He was used to such people. Somewhat impatiently, he explained that, under no circumstances, was he authorized to open the doors between stops and that, in any case, his inspector had been quite firm on the topic: all those on board were to remain there until both the transport company inspector and the police, now on their way, gave permission for them to leave.

Sara caught herself hoping they wouldn't be long. The heat in the motionless bus was already overpowering now that no cool breezes -- or draughts, depending on your point of view -- were blowing through the open windows. The realization that they were, at least temporarily, trapped in a closed space with a dead man had permeated the consciousness of even the slowest passenger, and the cries of protest were becoming shriller by the moment.

Images from various detective novels she had read --

and they were legion -- rose unbidden to her mind. She began to imagine hordes of fat blue flies settling on the decaying corpse at her feet, feeding on it, voraciously. In the books, they always seemed to come from nowhere, and she kept glancing nervously down, knowing that the first sight of a bluebottle would have her jumping up on the seat again and shouting with the others. Happily there appeared to be no blood, and for the moment the corpse was neither decaying, at least visibly, nor was it covered in winged scavengers.

The noise in the street echoed the cries within the bus, which, having skewed quite violently on braking, was now blocking at least half the traffic, and creating considerable confusion. Car horns were honking; irate drivers were shaking their fists in the air; the *cafés* were emptying as their patrons rushed out to add to the numbers already on the sidewalk in the expectation of witnessing a drama. At the stalls outside the grocery stores, gawping had taken precedence over shopping.

When a passenger shouted out the news about the murder, a look of gratification spread over most faces. More and more onlookers crowded round the stationary bus, standing on tiptoe, jostling those in front, some holding infants up in the air, others their cell phones, hoping to catch a glimpse or a shot of something, anything, desperate to capture some juicy detail to liven up the stories they would self-importantly be telling family and friends not just that evening but for days and weeks to come. I was there, I saw it, they would say, and I heard everything the inspector said. Look at my photos. Some of them might even be on the evening news, puffing about their shock, the decline of French society and the terrible immigrant problem.

Suddenly a familiar sound made itself heard over the turmoil in the street. The two-note siren of the French police. *Pim-pom, pim-pom, pim-pom.* Louder and louder. Reluctantly, the crowd parted like the Red Sea, to make way for the van, followed by an ambulance. The two vehicles came to an abrupt halt, one swerving to the front and one to the back of the bus. Several police men and women jumped out of the van, blowing whistles, shouting at the bystanders, vigorously clearing as much space as possible. Out of the ambulance jumped the stretcher-bearers, ready to move the body as soon as orders were given. One of the *policiers* rapped officiously on the door, calling out for the driver to open it. In vain. The driver affirmed his intention of keeping the doors shut until he received the appropriate orders from his inspector.

"This is the police, you *imbécile*," called the constable, forgetting his usual manners in the face of such obstinacy. The magic word had no effect, however, and the ensuing altercation, carried on at full pitch through the windows, enchanted all the spectators, not least the children, whose vocabulary was being enlarged with every passing second. Fortunately, the two protagonists were unable to come to blows. By now, the *policier* was beside himself, looking as if, at any minute, he might succumb to the combination of rage and heat and collapse on the spot. He was saved by the timely arrival of a small, rotund man in a navy blue uniform who identified himself as the long-awaited traffic inspector. He calmed everybody's spirits by requesting the driver to conform to police wishes. Immediately.

The front doors slid open; a breath of fresh hot air filled the bus. Several passengers threw themselves on to the steps in an attempt to leave. They were forestalled by a ring of policemen waiting to escort them all, one by one, into the van, where they would be expected to prove their identity and answer some questions. Probably they would have to repeat everything for the higher echelons who always came later. Sara's heart sank. If only she'd chosen somewhere else to sit. Or some other museum to visit. Or the underground as her mode of transport. If only... It was all too late now. She could foresee a long and difficult ending to a day that had seemed to begin so well.

CHAPTER TWO

Paris Story

"Your name is Thomas; you live in Montreal, Canada; you are a Canadian citizen, but you also have French nationality. Is that correct? You are a citizen of two countries at the same time?"

Obviously puzzled by the lack of clarity in Sara's *état civil*, her status in society, so to speak, the *commissaire*, introduced as Monsieur Santal, returned her identity card after all the particulars on it had been carefully noted. Sara was quite nervous about her possible answer. Should she rush to explain this proliferation of nationalities as perhaps a peculiarly Canadian phenomenon -- after all, some people she knew had as many as three or four -- or should she wait for the *commissaire* himself to pursue the topic. She could even discuss the whole migratory phenomenon that is so characteristic of the late XXth and early XXIst Centuries, mentioning in that context the former Governor General of Canada's problem with her dual citizenship.

Finally, she remembered her own advice never to volunteer information. She usually offered such advice, it was true, in reference to Customs -- and usually to the particularly unpleasant Canadian version thereof -- but it was always useful nevertheless. Sara then decided to let discretion be the better part of valour and wait for the questions. She knew they would come sooner or later.

Eighteen hours had gone by since a corpse had dropped into her lap. The day before, in a remarkably stuffy little van, the police had interviewed all the passengers before allowing them to go home. They were mainly interested in acquiring names and addresses, although, as usual, they were quick to look hard at the papers of anyone who looked as if he or she might have been born in a different country, particularly those on the southern shore of the Mediterranean. Apparently, disappointingly almost, no unauthorized residents were found, and the whole group was able to leave without difficulty.

The bus driver, still not resigned to missing the game on TV, had been questioned a little more closely. He remembered that the victim had got on somewhere near the

Porte de la Chapelle on the northern edge of Paris, but, naturally enough, had not noticed where he sat or who sat by him.

"The bus emptied later on, but at that point it was full; I'm paid to drive the bus and keep an eye out for freeloaders. I'm not paid to watch the passengers and see who sits where," he added belligerently. The bus driver was safe in the knowledge that his blonde hair and blue eyes would protect him from certain forms of harassment at least. "It's little enough pay we get for what we do; if you're going to try and hold us accountable for what passengers get up to once they're on the bus, then you can bet there's going to be a strike. I'm fed up with all this nonsense. And what's more I'm now on overtime. My shop-steward's going to hear about this harassment."

He was still grumbling when he finally left, abandoning his bus, the inspector having grudgingly promised he would send for a replacement to drive it back to the garage when the police were finished.

Sara's interview had naturally lasted somewhat longer than the others, since she had to satisfy the police, at least temporarily, that she had sat for a good while beside a dead man with a knife in his back without noticing anything in particular.

"You are quite sure, Madame," said one of the older men, "that at no time did you suspect that your neighbour on the back seat had been stabbed in the back?"

Put like that, it did seem odd. Sara felt prompted to reply that the only back she checked for knives on a regular basis was her own, but decided this was no time for humour of any kind.

"It never occurred to me, sergeant, to check whether I was sitting next to a corpse. I'm sorry if that sounds unlikely, but it's surely not something one expects on a bus in Paris." It sounded funny whether she meant it to or not.

"But, Madame, did you not find it strange that he sat there with his eyes closed all the time? You yourself said his head was lolling from side to side."

"That's what my husband does every evening, sergeant, when he comes home from work. He sits in the armchair for about half an hour with his eyes closed and his head lolling. I never assume he's been stabbed. I assume he's having a snooze before supper because he's had a hard day at the office. Mind you, I can see that my reaction may well be different next time he dozes off that way, particularly if there's no sound of snoring."

The interviewer dismissed her irrelevant domestic preoccupations. He could see the logic in her answers, but what appeared to be a certain flippancy left him somewhat dissatisfied. More explanations were definitely required.

"Madame, did it occur to you at any point to try to wake up this man who might have gone past his stop?"

"Well, of course it did. But it's always awkward to interfere like that. He could have told me to mind my own business. Particularly in Paris. In any case, if he was Hassidic, then of course he wasn't allowed to look at anybody. They can't raise their eyes, you know. At least, that's what people say. There was quite a fuss about it in Montreal at one point. So it was quite a dilemma, because..." Her voice tailed off as she saw the sergeant's eyes glaze over with incomprehension. Better anyway not to give the impression she knew too much.

"Well, why did you choose that seat? What made you go and sit beside him if you didn't know him?"

Would he have asked that particular question, she wondered, if the victim had not belonged to what are now called "visible minorities." Perhaps he thought it peculiar that she had not preferred someone more orthodox in the other sense of the word!

"Sergeant, I didn't deliberately sit beside him. I went to the back of the bus because I like sitting there; there's frequently more room than on the other seats. Also, I can see the other passengers more easily, and I enjoy watching the people around me. The corpse, no! no!, the person who turned out to be a corpse, just happened to be there at the same time." It didn't sound convincing to her either.

"What were you doing in the area where you got on the bus, Madame? On a hot day in Paris, what is the attraction? You are a tourist; you did not go there to work."

At least he wasn't assuming she was one of the ladies of easy virtue that tend to ply their trade in the neighbourhood where she had got on the bus. Perhaps she did look elderly after all, thought Sara with a pang. She debated briefly whether to tell him she regularly made a little pilgrimage to the nearby *Gare du Nord* because of the ballet and the books by Caryl Brahms and S. J. Simon, the two collaborators on a series of comic thrillers mainly published before the Second World War. She had adored them, the writers and the books, when she was still in her teens and continued in effect to adore them in her later years. In the end, thinking it better to be prudent, she decided to confine her response to safer topics like her visit to the French publishing firm in one of the smaller side streets.

"You are paid to translate books, Madame?" He could not have sounded more incredulous if he had tried. "What kind of books would that be?"

Her heart sank.

"Detective novels, Sergeant. Thrillers. Murder mysteries."

She half expected them to clap handcuffs on her straight away. The man's immediate jerk on hearing her answer seemed to indicate that his initial reaction had been to do just that, but probably the smirks on his colleague's faces deterred him somewhat. Or prudence prevailed.

With a sigh and a shake of his head, he dismissed her.

"Thank you, Madame, we will be in touch, should we need more information." Then turning to the young agent standing nearby, he instructed him to see Sara home.

The fresh-faced agent did indeed accompany her back to her small hotel on the rue Bonaparte, near *Saint-Sulpice* church, not, it transpired, from courtesy to a possible foreigner, but in order to confirm that she was in fact who she said she was and that she was staying where she said she was.

She almost suggested to him that he should visit the church itself while he was in the neighbourhood, to see the superb Delacroix frescoes tucked away in one of the chapels as well as the strip of brass that traversed the floor of the church near the altar and that was illuminated by the sun at exactly midday, solar time. Confronted by his lack of response, however, to her earlier chattier remarks about first the weather, then the annual poetry fair which took place every spring on the square itself, Sara decided against it.

In the event, after the hotel management had confirmed her statements, she went by herself to contemplate Saint Michael, Heliodoros and Jacob, the three Delacroix frescoes she had thought of recommending, as consolation for missing the Arab Institute and its delicate architecture. The frescoes reminded her that she owed another visit to the Louvre to see Delacroix's Women of Algiers once more before she left.

Such a voyeur, she thought, like so many male painters, always wanting to observe women, to capture them on canvas. He probably never spared a thought for the privacy of his subjects! But the beauty of the painting always submerged her. Sometimes she wanted to suggest they really should hang it beside Picasso's version of the same theme; at other times she decided she preferred to savour it by itself, although she had a little weakness also for Delacroix' painting of a similar situation in Montpellier.

Later that evening, after dining alone near Montparnasse in a cheap but good Lebanese restaurant where she knew the owners, she sat in a darkened cinema watching a very sombre but moving Algerian film about love and madness. Occasionally she wondered if the constable or another one like him had been instructed to follow her and if so, whether he (she?) was enjoying himself, and whether various superiors would draw any hasty conclusions from what she now realized might have been perceived, in the context, as an equivocal choice of entertainment.

Would they think that a liking for Lebanese cuisine

and an interest in Algerian movies, let alone her admiration for a painter who had lived in North Africa, might be connected to the death in suspicious circumstances of an orthodox Jew? Parlous times, indeed, if one had constantly to think in such divisive terms.

The dead man had invaded her sleep. Eyeless sockets sprang at her out of blackness; skeletons fell out of closets lining a long corridor; gleaming knives threatened her children, now small again. "Is this a dagger I see before me?" Macbeth stumbled down the long stone stairs, stretching out his hands to grasp her throat. She had awakened, hot and sweaty, heart thumping, to find her bedclothes tumbled on the floor, the glass beside her bed knocked over, water still dripping slowly over the edge. Only after a long bath and lots of *café crème* with croissants did she feel capable of thrusting away from her inner eye the haunting image of her temporary neighbour, of preparing once again to face the world.

Shortly after her breakfast, as she was walking out the door to go for a stroll, a tiny black and white police car pulled up. She was invited, politely but firmly, to accompany the driver and his companion to the *Police judiciaire*, the Criminal Police Department. Sara would have liked to leave a message with someone, to say where she was going, to have the security of knowing that one friendly person at least in Paris would be concerned about her welfare and make every effort to rescue her if necessary. The police didn't give any indication that they would encourage her to do so, however, and she didn't want to look ridiculous by dramatizing a situation that was probably quite mundane, quite anodyne in fact.

Somewhat reluctantly, therefore, she joined them. They sped off, along the boulevard Saint-Germain, down Saint-Michel onto *l'Ile de la Cité*, along the *boulevard du Palais*, with scarcely a glance for the spire of the *Sainte-Chapelle*. Over the Seine again, to scream to a halt not far from the spectacular *Hôtel de Ville* or City Hall, with its fountains playing away, in front of a rather disappointing, very functional building facing the river.

Nervously she followed her escort through drab, badly lit corridors, into an elevator that ground slowly upward. It was nothing like the friendly police stations of the Miss Marple tradition or the noisy confusion of the American TV precinct. The very ordinariness of everything surrounding her was Kafkaesque. She could almost feel herself giving a guilty start every time she heard a noise, rather as if she were a suspect being brought in by Janvier in an Inspector Maigret novel.

Would the police superintendant in real life also smoke a pipe? Did he too keep a bottle of cognac and some glasses in a cupboard for those who confessed from sheer exhaustion? These and other preoccupations she knew were due as much to her vivid imagination as to ignorance. They kept charging round her mind as the agents ushered her in to a small not totally unwelcoming office, although, in true French tradition, somewhat airless. Heaven protect us all, she thought, from those frightening *courants d'air*, the deadly draughts the French see and feel in every open window and every breeze.

The desk, which took up rather a lot of space, was

clearly either an antique or an extremely good fake and the bureaucratically beige walls were hung with what were surely reproductions of one or two paintings by Matisse as well as a few rather good black and white photographs. The *commissaire* had good taste.

The crowning glory, however, which she hoped most visitors were in a position to appreciate, was the huge window offering a splendid view along the river to the *façade* of Notre-Dame cathedral. It very much reminded her of the description she'd read in a French novel, by Hélène Parmelin she thought, such a great writer, in which a *commissaire* sits with his back turned to just such a window, and the twin towers of Notre Dame cathedral appear to be resting one on each shoulder.

But this was no novel, and the questioning had begun anew. *Commissaire* Santal, dressed in an expensive suit cut in the English manner, the waisted jacket emphasizing his slim build, was extremely courteous. So was the rotund transport inspector whom she recognized from his brief appearance the preceding day. Behind the courtesy, you were naturally aware not only of a firm commitment to solving this particular mystery but also of all the rather awesome power of the French state. Gone were the habeas corpus rules of the country she normally lived in; here until very recently you could consult a lawyer only after the process had gone on for some time.

"Perhaps, Madame Thomas, you would care to explain to me why you have two passports?" The question was asked in a gravelly voice, redolent of cigarette smoke and good wine.

The answer was disappointingly simple. Marriage. To a Canadian. Who in turn had acquired French citizenship some years earlier. The *commissaire* looked as if he would have preferred some more exotic reason or perhaps he did not approve of married women being allowed the same dual nationality privileges as men. Perhaps he went so far as to think the world was better off when women didn't have any nationality at all. He might even have had hopes, Sara thought wildly, of catching a latter-day Mata Hari in his net.

"You have told us, Madame, that you visited a publishing house which proposes to hire you to translate murder mysteries." His distaste or disbelief was only too evident, but whether his dissatisfaction was with her story or the nature of the books was not so easily determined. "But the bus you took afterwards is not one that leads you back to your hotel. What possible reason could you have had for taking it?"

"Well, one of the wonderful things about Paris is the number of museums and art galleries. When I'm here, I always try to visit as many as possible. Of course, without living here, one can never do them all, and sometimes the ones I really want to see are closed for repairs or restoration or something." Sara could hear herself babbling on but found it impossible to stop. "So, naturally, when I realized there was a bus going almost directly to the *Institut du monde arabe*, which I hadn't seen in years, well, it seemed a pity not to take advantage of it. There was just time to get there and have a couple of hours before closing..."

"Thank you." The *commissaire* cut in, somewhat overwhelmed by this Niagara pouring out at him. "And how long had you known the deceased?"

Taken aback as much by the interruption as by the question, Sara stared at him. Suddenly the meaning of the question struck home. "But, *commissaire*, I have already told you I didn't know him. Are you trying to trap me? That's a dirty trick. In any case, let me tell you it will take a better trap than that to catch me. Not," she added hastily, "that there's anything to catch. It's just a way of speaking."

Santal was a little startled to be addressed so frankly, and the transport inspector took advantage of the momentary silence to ask what had obviously been troubling him.

"Madame Thomas, your visit to Paris was, according to your statement, to have been relatively brief. Not more than three weeks. Yet you use a *Navigo*, a renewable bus pass. Is that not a waste of money? How do you explain it?"

Was wasting money worse or better than murder, Sara wondered, but decided to keep her question to herself. After her previous slight outburst, Sara was anxious to cooperate as much as was reasonably possible.

"It's just that I travel constantly when I'm in Paris. First of all, my friends are scattered all over the city, and I've told you that I try to take in as many museums as possible. Besides that, exploring unfamiliar areas is one of my favourite pastimes. And I always try to take the bus although it can be so expensive. You see so much more, and of course it's also safer. It's too bad that there aren't more of them in the evening. Anyway, even for only three weeks, it's cheaper for me to use a pass than to buy tickets any other way, even a weekly pass. There is another reason. I hope you won't find it silly." She was babbling again. "When you have a *Navigo*, you feel like a real Parisian, not like a summer tourist. It's very thrilling for me to click it as I go past the bus driver. It gives me the impression..."

The inspector too cut her off with a brief thank you. Nevertheless her remarks about Paris, no matter how silly they sounded, perhaps because they sounded silly and "typically feminine," had brought an irritatingly indulgent smile to both men's faces, a smile that disappeared when Santal renewed his questioning.

Several hours of this left Sara absolutely drained. The *commissaire* had sent for coffee and pastries while he took her over and over the same ground, experimenting with different hypotheses about her involvement, speculating constantly about her national identity -- clearly the two passports still bothered him. There finally came a point when she could no longer function, and Santal, expressing somewhat belated concern for the welfare of a visitor to France's shores, decided to let her go.

"For now," he specified. "We may find it necessary, *chère Madame*," he was full of solicitude, "to pursue this conversation, possibly even with the *juge d'instruction*, the examining magistrate; but we must all hope the matter will be settled soon. Please do not move from your hotel. *À bientôt.*"

The air and the sunshine glinting off the Seine were a welcome relief from the stuffiness of Monsieur Santal's office and made Sara decide to walk along the *quais* until she should come to the place Dauphine where she would sit under the chestnut trees and treat herself to a very late, and preferably relaxing, lunch.

It wasn't, of course, to be quite so simple. The *bouquinistes* were all out and the parapets overlooking the river seemed to groan under the weight of their open boxes, invitingly displaying books for every taste and pocket. Tourists and natives alike were rummaging through the piles in the hope of finding, perhaps a first edition, perhaps an out-of-print book, perhaps merely a cheap paperback. Sara never could resist, and she too progressed from stall to stall, scrutinizing titles as she went. This was how she had picked up her collection of early French feminist novelists from the turn of the previous century.

Fleetingly, as she paused to admire a very handsome edition of *Germaine de Staël's Corinne*, an image of the "rabbi's" plastic bag flashed across her mind, causing her to wonder whether his books had not in fact been bought at some second-hand bookstall, specializing perhaps in Hebrew. She would mention it to Santal at their next meeting. She would also ask him if the dead man was indeed a rabbi. Oddly enough, the *commissaire* had not mentioned any details about him that morning, beyond asking if she knew him. Surely, information should always be a two-way street.

Suddenly Sara stopped dead in her tracks. Antony! Her favourite Romantic play by her favourite Romantic nineteenth-century author, Alexandre Dumas. It was almost never re-issued and correspondingly almost impossible to find. Her own copy had disappeared several years earlier, probably borrowed by another Dumas freak. It was one of the few Romantic dramas with good parts for women, although once again the heroine dies at the end. But at least she had fun beforehand! "*Elle me résistait. Je l'ai assassinée.*" What a great closing line and how plausibly he lied! What a pity it was never staged nowadays. She paid over a not inconsiderable number of euros and went off happily clutching her treasure, her day redeemed.

CHAPTER THREE

Casque D'or

Relaxing as planned at a *café-terrasse* on the place Dauphine, in the shade of the chestnut trees, now, alas, minus their spring candles, Sara caught herself staring at the door of le Moulin. That was the affectionate name given to the apartment where Simone Signoret and, of course, Yves Montand had lived when in Paris. If she scrunched up her eyes, she could just imagine Simone stepping out, smiling at the neighbours, stopping perhaps to sign an autograph or two, then heading off, to a political meeting maybe, or to the studios for a movie she was filming. Incredibly beautiful even to the raddled end. And always so utterly intelligent. And, as it turned out, a good writer too.

Sara shook herself slightly. All this dreaming wouldn't bring anyone back. And there were other dead people to worry about. Slowly sipping her wine, she wondered how the inquiry into the rabbi's death was progressing and what the police thought her role might be, if they thought about her at all.

Surely they could not seriously imagine she was involved. Sara knew that if you were suspected of murder in France, the authorities could keep you in jail without trial for incredibly long periods. These could last up to two or three years, possibly more, while they investigated not only the crime but every incident in your entire life, including the time at school you put glue onto the pigtails of the girl sitting in front of you or dipped them into your portable inkwell. Not a pleasing prospect.

In spite of the odd flash of uncertainty or anxiety, however, she did not truly find it possible to believe the police would ever consider her a major suspect. But then, she also did not find it possible to believe she was involved in a real murder. It seemed to her occasionally almost as if they were all players on a stage set, in the opening scene, say, of a French version of a traditional English mystery, *Sleuth* for instance.

Yet it was real enough for the victim and, one supposed, would be one day for the murderer too. Not to worry. Like the Mounties, in the end the French police probably got their man -- or woman -- and didn't waste time on middle-aged translators with a large bump of curiosity.

The dessert arrived just at that point. *Pêche cardinal*, poached peaches with raspberry sauce. Perfect for a hot summer's day. The spoon slid easily between the almond slivers and through the fresh raspberry coulis, then sliced through the firm but tender flesh of the gently poached fruit. Sara savoured every flavourful mouthful before ordering the espresso coffee that would put the finishing touch to a delicious meal that could easily have been included in a gourmet magazine. *Concombre à l'antiboise*, peeled, seeded and blanched cucumber stuffed with tuna and mayonnaise, then *poulet à la Sainte-Ménéhould*, rather more complicated with its trussed legs inside the chicken, bathing in a delicious sauce, followed by a selection of cheeses and her dessert. And, to accompany the whole, a bottle of *Apremont*, in memory of a delightful holiday in Savoy, on the lakeshore at Annecy, where not a balcony in summer was bare of flowers. For a moment she wondered through the pleasant glow whether she shouldn't have settled for half a bottle. Fortunately it was too late to go back on her decision. What Renaissance Italian cardinal was it who said that it was better to have sinned and regret it than not to have sinned and regret that? Good advice, anyway.

Sara spent the rest of the afternoon in the gardens of the *Palais royal*. There she shopped for some extra presents to take home for a few friends and for her occasional typist, as well as, in what had to be one of the best toyshops anywhere, some gifts for that evening's hostess, or rather her two children. It seemed as if all the games of her own childhood were on display and, oddly enough, most of them still charmed the latest generations.

The small striped columns by Buren were still in the courtyard near the Ministry of Finance and really, with time, they had become more and more acceptable, although it would probably always be difficult to consider them either as sculpture or any form of art. One wanted to put a vase on top or a large aspidistra plant or cross the courtyard by jumping from one to another. The youngsters nearby obviously enjoyed throwing coins into the subterranean fountain; in fact, most people stopped to gaze down over the railings at the flowing stream. A universal attraction, Sara thought, watching moving water. Ole Man River, he just keeps rollin' along.

Much later, after a long soak in her hotel bathroom, she started primping, as she liked to call it, for her evening outing, dinner with some old friends. A plain black dress, she thought, with the jazzy new brooch she had bought a few days before in a little store behind the *Galeries Lafayette* and the gold-coloured Italian sandals she had picked up near the *Châtelet*, an ancient area in the centre of Paris she loved to walk in. The fountain was so beautiful, as is the statue of Victory. So much to be admired in just one public square. Anyway, all that, she hoped would make up for her hair which was succumbing to the heat and humidity of Paris.

Finally, as ready as she would ever be, she took a taxi to her destination, a minute apartment -- two quite small rooms and a corridor converted into a bathroom and laundry -- that had been most ingeniously arranged to make the most of the available space. The ceilings were very high, as the building itself dated back to the late sixteenth-century, and her friends had built three loggias, if that was the right word, a hanging kitchen, bedroom and workspace, in the larger room where they lived most of the time, as well as a second hanging bedroom in the other to accommodate the children who thus had some floor space to play or work on.

Her host and hostess, senior civil servants, were old friends in spite of the age difference, Hélène being some sixteen years younger than Sara. They had met in Montreal approximately twenty years earlier. The former, an exchange student at the university where Sara occasionally taught, as a part-time instructor, a course in translation theory, had sat in on Sara's class, and a mutual passion for thrillers had cemented the budding friendship. Hélène had acted as baby-sitter for the older woman's children who, in turn, had, much later, each spent a year in France being an au pair girl for their former baby-sitter. When Hélène had married Éric, a co-worker, the two husbands had fortunately developed the same warm regard for each other.

Both Hélène and Éric were *énarques,* that superior breed of French civil servants, graduates of the *École nationale d'administration*, the National School of Administrative Studies, who achieve their status by surviving what is probably the most competitive and grueling education system in the world.

To round out the evening, they had invited two other couples, all also *énarques*. Sara had already met Marielle and Vincent, both still in their twenties and, in their casually elegant clothes, looking more like students than career functionaries. Vincent came from a town in eastern France but Marielle belonged to that minority of minorities, she was a Parisian born and bred.

Joël and Françoise, both of a slightly older generation, were new to Sara. Joël was originally from Martinique but had spent all his adult life in France. He and Françoise had met in the northern working-class suburb of Paris where she was born and where his parents had immigrated when they realized their son would be going to university in the metropolis.

They had both been standing in a line-up in the post office, they explained, waiting to buy stamps, when a sudden thunderstorm caused the lights to go out temporarily. In the ensuing panic, they had spoken to each other and had never looked back. The group spent some time over drinks chatting in this manner before settling down to their meal. As frequently happened in Paris, it was after nine-thirty by the time they actually took their seats around the tiny table. And, as usual, Sara was fascinated by the idea of people who started eating just when many North Americans were thinking in terms of going to bed.

She had been looking forward to telling Hélène and Eric her tale. Just the process of turning it into a story to relate would give her a better perspective on the events, exorcize them in a way. She also knew they would greet her experience with warm sympathy and concern for her well-being. They and their other guests were quite fascinated by the adventure, and after various expressions of support, most of the evening was spent embroidering ever more farfetched stories to account for the murder.

"I know. The books weren't real. Actually they were boxes filled with heroine, no, smack. No-one would stop a rabbi to look for drugs. A rival gang found out and stabbed him, but before they could grab the loot, you arrived." Hélène was jubilant.

"Oh, not drugs, Hélène. Everyone thinks of drugs. It's so obvious." Joël, seated on her right, seemed otherwise very taken with the smuggling end of her suggestion. "Why not something more classy? Wouldn't stamps do? Wasn't there an article in one of last week's newspapers about stamps disappearing? That's right. Two Penny Royals disappeared in Germany last week. There you are. He traded in stolen stamps. And he kept them between the leaves of the books, which were in fact real."

"Stamps are boring. Only specialists know anything about them." Hélène returned to the attack. "If you don't like drugs, what about paintings? They're classy enough. Only canvases, not frames, of course. A couple of miniatures were taken from a museum in Bologna quite recently. I'll bet he did regular runs and everything ended up in New York or California or even Japan, where the real money is. Anyway, it was still the work of a rival gang."

"Calm down, *chérie*. One would think we were watching an American TV series. Do you really have to invent a gangland killing just to explain away what happened to the poor man?" Eric had always been the more pedestrian of the two and was accustomed to pooh-poohing her more exotic flights of fancy.

Vincent, sitting opposite Sara, was obviously an Eric Ambler or John Le Carré type.

"What about Russian spies? Or he could have been working for the Israelis. No, it would be better if he were working for the Russians. Just because there's no Iron Curtain doesn't mean there's no spying, you know. For a start, there's all that industrial espionage, which must be much more important now than it was before. But let's say he was working for the Israelis. A double or triple agent. Many countries would pay well to know what nuclear arsenal Israel might have. Or, given that nothing has really changed in the Middle East, some of the Arab countries, I suppose. Anyway, the books Sara mentioned probably contained microdots on the cover page. Say the Israelis found out and killed him, because he had discovered the latest information concerning their atomic weapons. You know how uptight they are about that. Somebody's serving a life sentence, I think, for revealing they had the bomb."

"Oh, but it could just as easily have been the Iraqis or the Saudis, because no-one is supposed to know they've got the bomb." Unexpectedly, Eric had joined in.

Françoise, on his left, had her own ideas.

"I think he was involved in a plot to overthrow our own government. Nobody absolutely knows for a fact that he was Jewish. It's really a right-wing plot, and they used him, disguised that way, because then no-one would suspect him of being part of a Fascist-type uprising. Only the secret services found out, you know, the *défense du territoire*, Homeland Security lot, and they decided to get rid of him without the expense of a trial."

All the government employees around the table pretended to be shocked by such calumnies about their Masters, but while they were still light-heartedly if self-consciously arguing about its likelihood, Marielle, Vincent's wife, won the prize for the most inventive story of the evening, by developing a whole theory about visitors from outer space.

"You see, it's just like the woman in *My Stepmother is an Alien*. The extra-terrestrial wants to be among us and study us, but makes a mistake. Instead of imitating someone who'll pass unnoticed in any crowd, he or she, or whatever space beings are, read a book about the Russian or the Greek Orthodox church and turned him or herself etcetera into a pope, but landed in Paris instead of Athens. So, naturally, the others had to correct the situation. But they couldn't just waft this guy up, because even Sara would have noticed a disappearance or an assumption, if that's the right word, so they pretended to kill him, left the body there and took whoever was in it back up on a flying saucer!"

Loud groans greeted Marielle's effort, but they all had to admit she had a good imagination.

Sara was to remember many of these suggestions the following day, during her second interview with Santal. No police car was sent this time; an early telephone call summoned her to the office of the *juge d'instruction*, the examining magistrate, in the *Palais de justice* itself, a rather more elegant building than the previous one, but hardly more friendly. And certainly damper. She was pleased that she had thought of paying a short visit beforehand to the nearby *Quai des fleurs* in order to admire the massed colours and scents of the flowers on display. That at least started the day off on a cheerful note.

At the main gates, a police escort was assigned to her; on the walk through the corridors, unsurprisingly long, narrow and badly lit, Sara was quite startled, in fact upset, to pass several people, including one woman, who wore handcuffs. It was a very different experience from seeing it on the screen; her heart skipped a beat at the thought of the humiliation and sense of powerlessness involved.

She noticed too that the attitude of their police escorts was very different from hers, as if being a prisoner, even if still technically innocent, suddenly made people less human. The guards said "*tu*" to those wearing handcuffs and called them by their first names or used nicknames. Sara thought she couldn't have borne to be treated with such lack of respect and, in spite of the flowers, was already quite indignant by the time she reached her destination.

The *commissaire* introduced her to the magistrate, a remarkably young man, visibly from the upper classes, B.C.B.G (bon chic, bon genre) as the French would have said, although she really appreciated the "Hooray Henry" used by the Brits. He gravely explained his role to her.

"Normally, Madame, I do not intervene so early in the investigation. It is, you understand, the *commissaire*'s task to hunt down the criminals. Here, however, we are concerned that the case might have certain -- overtones."

"Overtones?" This from Sara.

"Yes. I will explain. The -- er -- deceased, although a French citizen, yes, yes, definitely a French citizen," his hesitation made him sound as if he regretted the fact, "belongs to a -- er -- group, no, a community, which has in the past, alas we must add, often been the victim of, of, of..."

"Racist attacks?" It was Sara's turn to cut in.

"Er, yes, we could say that, although I must add that France, of course, does not distinguish between its citizens, attaches the same importance to all our compatriots, whatever their colour or religion, and does its best to discourage feelings or, or behaviour of such an unpleasant nature."

Not during the Second World War and the Nazi occupation, you didn't. Although tempted, Sara was careful not to make the remark out loud. It would have been counterproductive. Besides, the magistrate was too young to have been in any way responsible. He looked as if he'd barely had time to graduate. But, if the case was touchy, they would surely not have given it to a beginner. He must be older than he seemed. Unless they could use his youth as an excuse if he boobed. That was always a possibility.

"So, you see," added the magistrate, "we are concerned about the, should I say, political dimensions the case may have. That is why I am already helping my colleague, who is naturally more than competent to deal with the case himself," he added, most tactfully.

Santal sat stony-faced throughout this exchange. All the tact in the world couldn't change the fact that the direction of the enquiry had, to all intents and purposes, been taken out of his hands because someone on high had been less concerned with the solution than with its possible effect on voting patterns or popularity polls. Now, however, he picked up the questioning from the day before. A little half-heartedly at first, like someone going through the motions, in no way as if he were interested in the answers but as if he were merely repeating the questions so that the magistrate could hear for himself what she had to say.

Sara was irrationally relieved by the discussion so far, because it gave her the impression that she at least was eared of all suspicion. She readily confirmed her previous statements about her identity, her profession, her reasons for being in Paris and for taking that particular bus. She added a few complimentary remarks about the Arab Institute and its site on the banks of the Seine.

"You have many Arab friends, it would seem, Madame."

The question, or statement, came at her out of left field. So, they had indeed followed her to her Lebanese restaurant and her Algerian movie, she thought, as well as noting her intended destination on the previous day, and drawn all the wrong conclusions. Perhaps they were even now checking up on her civil service friends, to see if they all belonged to the same conspiracy! So much for being reassured by the initial discussion. Her response was a laconic "yes"; it seemed wise in the circumstances.

"It sometimes happens," Santal was being cautious, "that Arabs entertain anti-Jewish feelings."

"During the Second World War, Morocco was the only occupied country besides Denmark to protect its Jewish citizens."

"You are well informed," the *juge d'instruction* intervened.

"I have always been concerned with injustice in any form, and the Holocaust or Shoah would certainly come under that heading, would it not? To measure the full horror of what happened elsewhere, you have to know that some people or nations managed to resist and it was therefore possible to do so. You get a different perspective then." With this repugnantly smug statement, Sara had broken her promise to herself and brought up the German occupation of France, however indirectly. During their embarrassed silence, she decided to get in a question of her own.

"I assume from what you're saying that the dead man was Jewish. Was he also a rabbi?"

"He was, we understand, at rabbinical school and so potentially a rabbi. Why do you ask?" Somewhat to her surprise, Santal answered the question.

"Plain curiosity, you could say. You know my living comes from translating mystery novels, so it's natural for me to want to know more details about a crime that actually involves me in some way. But I did want to make a suggestion about his books. They looked very old, possibly valuable, yet he was carrying them in an ordinary plastic bag. That seemed odd to me until I purchased a book on the *quais* yesterday and was given a plastic bag to carry it in. Do you think he might just have bought them at a flea market or some other second-hand bookstore? If you're interested in retracing his footsteps, that might help you."

"Yes, thank you," said Santal in an indulgent tone. "But we have thought of that. This is not, *chère Madame*, a detective novel, nor are you a private eye able to outwit both the murderer and the police. We are highly trained and very competent, even if our skills are not always recognized in high places." This with a sideways glance at the examining magistrate. "We have put out a call, and our agents are at this very moment interviewing one or two booksellers, including one from the *Marché aux puces*, our Flea Market, at *Clignancourt* who specializes in such books."

"Yes, of course. From there, the rabbi-to-be could have got on that bus that goes all the way round the outskirts of Paris, the *petite ceinture*, you know the one, and changed on to ours at *La Chapelle*. Perhaps there was something in the books, a secret message, or they were intended for some other buyer and were sold to him by mistake." Sara was off and running, like her friends at the dinner-party, if a little less wildly.

"Madame, Madame." The *commissaire* was losing patience. "I say again that this is not one of your books to translate. There was a piece of paper in one of them, with a list of names, but they mean nothing to us. Who is to know, anyway, who put it there and how long ago."

Sara felt like asking at least if the paper had yellowed with time or looked still fresh, but Santal was continuing.

"Our victim, as a mark of respect for the dead, we could perhaps give him his name, we have discovered it is Joseph Fainsilber. Monsieur Fainsilber, as I was saying, was a highly respected member of his community. It seems nothing in his private life could warrant any suspicions of illicit behaviour."

"But I'm not accusing him of any such thing. It just seems to me that he could have been killed by mistake because he got the wrong books." Sara was quite indignant.

"I assure you, Madame Thomas," the *juge d'instruction* again, "that all avenues will be pursued. We are currently interested, nevertheless, in the possibility that this is not murder, *un crime crapuleux*, but some form of political assassination, in which case three particular groups spring to mind. Although of course there might be others."

The *commissaire* coughed as if to warn his colleague that he was talking too much, but to no avail.

"Monsieur Fainsilber had just returned from a trip to Israel. We must consider then that his activities may have been perceived to be Zionist, and that clandestine terrorist groups from the Near East might then have decided to eliminate him. Alternatively, the aggressors could be uncontrolled members, either of a political party that I do not care for or of a group of, of, skinheads." His repulsion was obvious. "That is why I should like to return to the question of your frequentations. If you are to be eliminated as a suspect, then we must be satisfied that you are completely innocent. You will admit that such questions must be clarified. Who are your friends?"

This was sounding more and more like the dinner party discussion of the night before, although skinheads and terrorists had never surfaced. "Some of my best friends..." she almost responded, but then decided they might not be familiar with the context. They could hardly be suggesting that she was a skinhead's moll, and nothing would have made her speak knowingly to a member of the nameless far-right political party, so she decided to concentrate her response on the remaining element in the magistrate's discourse.

A lengthy discussion ensued, which allowed Sara, or so she believed, to convince both men that friendship with individuals of one national, ethnic or religious persuasion -- or belonging oneself to such a group -- does not necessarily imply hatred of other individuals of different persuasions. Political Science 100, she thought. In her case, it would have worked both ways in any case. Did having friends who happened to be Jewish mean that she was necessarily hostile to Arabs or Muslims? And vice-versa?

"It really is outrageous," she concluded, "that people should think in such categories. "

Eventually, after signing a statement, Sara was allowed to leave. The atmosphere in the office had warmed up considerably by then, and she was not surprised to receive a message the following day informing her that she was free to return to Montreal. The boys in blue back home must have turned in a clean bill of health for her, she decided. No terrorist or right-wing connections for our respectable Sara. What a relief!

CHAPTER FOUR

Home Run

Sara's return flight was, as the saying goes, uneventful if not particularly pleasant. At best, air travel did not enchant her. Airports did not have the romantic associations of railway stations. You could not, for instance, lean out of the train window as the immortal Flora Poste did in her favourite novel, Cold Comfort Farm by Stella Gibbons, to wave at the loved ones you left behind, shouting: "Don't forget to feed the parrot!" to which, of course, there was still only one reply.

At airports you were whisked away along long corridors, through metal detectors, past surly attendants. You had to carry your own flight bags, wait for what seemed hours in dreary waiting rooms where no fresh air had ever been. There was never enough space in the plane, again always too little oxygen. She resented having to draw down the blind over her porthole because every airline company insisted on showing frequently inane movies to its captive audience. To boot, she had chosen a bad day, the one when there was no business class. It was first class or tourist with nothing in between. That meant the food was worse than usual, consisting essentially of what could only be described as a plastic snack. Fortunately, she had remembered to bring her own apple.

Reading occupied most of her journey. It was the only activity that made so many hours of enforced immobility bearable. A fast reader, Sara had armed herself with the latest issue of a translation journal, a travel diary from the Thirties translated into French by the author herself - a task not without its own hazards, as Beckett would confirm - and, reluctantly, a thriller from South Africa about a psychiatrist turned detective. Given her recent experience, she had been afraid such literature would pall, but she was soon absorbed in the highways and byways of this political analysis of a machinery of oppression from which, at the moment of writing at least, no one was apparently ever to escape. That led her to a brief but sombre meditation on the theme of "*plus ça change, plus c'est la même chose*"; her meditation was, however, followed by happier thoughts about the changes which had in fact already taken place, even though the whole journey would probably take many more years to complete.

Her neighbours seemed perfectly pleasant, but Sara deterred them as best she could from pursuing a conversation. Much as she enjoyed observing people on buses and on the streets, she hated the long enforced proximity of the airplane and felt that sharing an elbow rest was not conducive to civilized conversation. Total silence turned out to be almost impossible. Sara's bright and chatty right-hand neighbour insisted on telling her at what seemed to be great length about her visit to the *Musée d'Orsay*, the fascinating Left Bank museum that had originally been the splendid *Gare d'Orsay*, a *Beaux-Arts* railway station first opened in 1900. She had ended by asking Sara if she had managed to squeeze in any museum trips. Sara pondered for a moment whether she should say that her plans had been thwarted by murder; the temptation to watch the expression on her neighbour's face was great. In the end, discretion intervened and, shaking her head, she returned with manifest determination to her book, thus squelching further chitchat.

The plane arrived on time and made a smooth landing. Her husband, Victor, a tallish, quite good-looking man, with greying hair and gentle brown eyes, definitely in the friendly bear category, was waiting patiently at the airport. When possible, they always met each other after a long trip like the one Sara had just completed, even though it meant taking time off work.

Passing through Canadian Immigration and Customs

was normally such an unpleasant experience, reminiscent of the old Berlin Wall, that both felt the need to be welcomed after the ordeal by a particularly friendly face. Mind you, the procedure was getting, dare one say, easier, now that they had introduced electronic reporting posts. Just a question of ticking off a few boxes, entering some information and showing the Customs officer the print out the machine spewed out. Definitely had the long lines moving much faster. Even so, it was still exhausting after a long transatlantic flight. Probably after any flight for that matter.

Given her recent adventures it wasn't surprising really, that instead of the electronic posts, she was asked to get in the line that had her go to the Customs kiosk where she was questioned not by a machine, but by an agent. Once again, Sara had to explain her reasons for having left Canada, although, confronted by this reception, she preferred as usual to wonder about her reasons for coming back. Once again she had to explain how she spent her own money while abroad. Once again she resented the Uriah Heep attitude returning travellers were forced to assume in the attempt, not always successful, to propitiate the powers-that-be in their little boxes. She dreamed of having the energy to start a class action suit against them or to challenge their power under the Charter of Human Rights. God knows, they had more power than any police force. How odd that so many countries should choose to present their least attractive face to travellers!

Then, to cap it all off, after retrieving her luggage, she was waved into the Custom's pen, where she was asked to open both her suitcases. It looked as if the officer was having a bad day. He kept his comments to a minimum and did not return her smile. Both his French and his English sounded quite sketchy to Sara. He seemed to find the many books she had brought back more worthy of suspicion than her six pairs of newly-purchased shoes. He commented upon them at such length that Sara was hard put to decide whether, books being unfamiliar to him, he thought they were in themselves subversive elements or whether, as in Vincent's joking version of the rabbi to-be's death, he suspected the presence of microdots on the cover pages. After staring at the printed pages for some time -- probably uncomprehendingly, she thought nastily -- he finally returned them to the suitcases and released her to enter her own country.

"Again?" Victor asked. "I saw you pick up your suitcases; you were among the first, and, bingo, you disappeared from view. This is getting to be a habit. A bad one. You and whoever's in there are going to have to stop meeting this way!

"You know there are certain people they pick on. At least, according to the telly, that's what someone's research showed. And the certain people include women travelling alone. Unless we go on organized tours, we're not allowed out without a male escort. Canada is certainly no exception to the rule, although the situation has improved somewhat. That's why they keep stopping me. I could bear it if it were for a *rendez-vous galant* but no such luck, alas. No flirting, no passes come my way. Maybe it's my good taste in clothing and footwear has them thinking I am worthy of further inspection?"

"That only speaks to their good taste, my dear. But you see." Her husband smiled at her. "You should have taken me with you in your suitcase. Did they find anything? Were you caught smuggling something dreadful? A Picasso in the lining of your suitcase?"

"Don't joke," Sara snapped. "Sorry to react like that, but I told you what happened to me in Paris. The thought of being suspected of anything illegal makes me very nervous. The police are much more daunting when you're on the wrong end than when you're calling to complain about the noise made by the hard rock band the neighbouring kids have just started. Believe me."

"Of course, darling. Welcome back anyway. We'll drive home; you can have a rest, and then tell me all about it over a glass of champagne. You didn't give me any details over the phone, just a few cryptic remarks about a body on the bus, with a hint of more to come. Congratulations on your contract, by the way. Does that mean we can afford a winter holiday in the south?"

"Only if I get the stuff finished. And frankly, the books are so bad, it's going to be a major effort. It's extremely difficult, you know, to translate something that's badly written. People don't realize that. They think translating Proust or Virginia Woolf is tough, and that's true enough. But it's an exciting challenge rather than a chore. When the original makes no sense, and you have to render it into another language, it's rather like playing Blind Man's Bluff in a maze." She changed the subject, knowing she had a tendency to rant about such irritating topics. "How are the cats?"

LAST STEP

"Don't be surprised if they ignore you. The first week, they wandered everywhere looking for you; then they decided they'd been abandoned and went through their orphan routine. Now they've apparently adjusted to their single-parent status and may not want to return to the old arrangement! We'll see. In the meantime, tell me what movies you saw in Paris. It'll come as no surprise to learn there's not much on here, unless you like dubbed Italian films."

Chatting in this desultory manner and luckily avoiding the rush-hour build-up, they made their way back into the city. The car advanced on one of those typical Quebec autoroutes, stripped on either side of all life. The scenery that some trees might have helped to cover up was extraordinarily uninteresting and unattractive. She was so happy that Victor had decided to exit the autoroute and take Lakeshore road because she loved the west end suburbs, the beautiful homes along the water, and the spectacular scenery.

Seeing the stretch of glistening water, with the sun glancing off it, and little sailboats dotted here and there, Sara finally realized she was home. Subconsciously in France, she missed the sense of space and the knowledge that water was never far away. Once in Quebec, of course, she missed other things. Geographic space on the one hand, historical space on the other. *C'est la vie*, she thought without any particular claim to originality.

When the streets of Montreal replaced the awful suburban-cum-industrial sprawl that lay to the west of the city, she felt again that sense of displacement that inhabited her after every absence of more than a few days. Everything was just as she had left it, and yet changes had taken place. The trees were greener, flower baskets hung from most of the lampposts, the lawns had grown more velvety, and the children's street games had progressed to match the season.

On her block, the *À vendre*/For Sale sign in front of a roomy and attractive duplex was emblazoned with a sticker that said *Vendu*/Sold, but another house, single family this time, had now been put up for sale. The owners were friends of hers, and Sara was upset to think they were moving away, hoped they were not going far.

Her husband noticed her reaction. "Yes, I thought I'd save the news till you got back. There seemed no point in perhaps depressing you while you were in Paris. Charles and Vera have decided to retire. They've bought a house in the South of France, a bit off the beaten track, and will spend six months of the year there and six months in a *pied-à-terre* they've acquired in the downtown area."

"When was all this decided? I haven't been away all that long, barely a month. They hadn't mentioned a thing."

"Well, they've had their eye on that place in the Languedoc for ages, you knew that. Apparently, it came on the market very suddenly, so they had to make up their minds p.d.q. Right then Charles was offered a sweetheart deal if he retired early, Vera couldn't bear the thought of another winter in our climate, so they're off. Not to worry. It'll give us somewhere else to stay on our holidays!"

The car pulled into their driveway. The house, an Edwardian red-brick fronted by very elegant bow windows and set well back from the street, was shaded by one of the last elm trees to survive in Montreal. Every time she went past, Sara stroked it and spoke to it caressingly, as if such tender loving care would help to avert the evil eye of Dutch elm disease. The flowerbeds along the path to the front door and underneath the living-room window looked well-tended. She smiled to herself, imagining the hasty last-minute activity that had preceded her return.

In her rush to greet her home, Sara sped up the steps, leaving Victor to bring in the suitcases. The house was cool and quiet. She spent a few minutes wandering round, touching a few objects, moving a bibelot, and some of her larger chachkas here and there, doing what a friend of hers called her "Mrs. Tiggywinkle routine," taking psychological repossession of her home. The two cats, of the Heinz 57 varieties tradition, one mainly black, the other piebald, were lounging in the hallway. They took one look at her, swung silently around and stalked insolently away, in unison, their tails standing straight into the air, rather as if they had been rehearsing the move for days.

A cup of something hot seemed called for before anything further could be undertaken or consumed, and a very few minutes later, she and Vincent were sitting in the kitchen, looking out at their tiny garden and savouring the best tea she had drunk in weeks.

"I missed you, and I missed all this," Sara said, "but I know in a little while I'll be itchy for Paris again. Can't we do what Charles and Vera have done? You know, have the best of all possible worlds?"

"I'm working on it," came the answer. "What do you think I buy lottery tickets for? I've tried digging for gold in the garden, but no luck. While we're waiting for the millions, go and have your siesta. The girls are coming over later. You'll need to be bright-eyed and bushy-tailed, because they won't be satisfied until they've squeezed out of you every detail of what happened in Paris. And I'll be backing them up."

For a while, Sara lay on her bed and watched the leaves on the branches dancing outside her window. Victor's pyjamas had been thrown across the back of a chair. She could see that, in her absence, he'd been gradually encroaching on her space, moving her hairbrush to one side, piling up his books where she normally kept hers. She smiled. It was good to be in a human room again after the anonymity of a hotel.

Gradually she relaxed, until her eyes closed, and she drifted off into a light but slightly uneasy slumber. It was peopled by juggling flight attendants tossing drinks to each other from aisle to aisle over the helpless heads of the passengers, youngsters playing *Le jeu de l'oie*, the very European or perhaps Middle Eastern Goose Game, while their parents warned them against microdots, a policeman arresting her for reading books.

Two hours later, she did wake up refreshed, however, and a shower and shampoo completed the transformation. Hearing voices from the living room, she slipped quickly into a long cotton dress she kept for relaxing at home and went hastily downstairs where she was greeted effusively by both her daughters.

After an initial embrace, Claire, the elder of the two, a member of the production staff of a national TV show, held her mother at arm's length, in order, she said, to examine her for traces of criminal activity. Blond and curly-haired, with blue eyes and dimples, she was taller and narrower of build than her mother, looked younger than her thirty-one years. She dressed in colourful exotic clothes and got away with it. Sara always said Claire was a throwback to her maternal great grandmother, a strong-minded village midwife and general witch.

Emma held on to her mother rather longer, as if to protect her against some unknown danger. Slightly younger than Claire, not quite thirty, she was the manager of a small private business and looked much the same as she had ten years earlier. Red-haired and broad-shouldered, she was never less than elegant, and somehow managed to get the inside track on forthcoming fashions before almost anybody else in Quebec. At first glance, she appeared more conservative than her elder sister, but a second look revealed the personal flair in the choice of accessories that gave her a special distinction. Emma took after her paternal grandmother, a quiet determined woman who had managed to become a lawyer in spite of family opposition to the higher education of women.

It was odd that two sisters who were in fact so different, in character and in physique, could at the same time resemble each other to such an extent that people who knew one of them could recognize the other on the street, even mistake one for the other.

Victor had prepared something light to eat, a little caviar, a few slices of smoked salmon, a most deliciously rich hare *pâté*, an assortment of cheeses, some salad and fruit.

Not your average supper; perhaps he wanted to ease the transition, perhaps it was his way of saying welcome home. Claire and Emma had brought some yummy pastries. Before settling down to the table, however, they first cracked open a bottle of champagne to celebrate Sara's return to the fold. After distributing her presents: perfume, earrings and feminist journals for her daughters, some music and a scarf for her husband, she found herself retelling the story of the dead rabbi-to-be, her evening with Hélène and Éric, the meetings with the *commissaire* and the *juge d'instruction*. The worst part, she said, was having her fingerprints taken. So humiliating. She shuddered as she said it, remembering how violently she had scrubbed her hands afterwards to remove all memory of the operation.

Later, over their supper, the discussion continued.

"Poor Mummy," said Emma, anxious, "you must have been terrified when you realized he was dead. Did you really scream?"

"Never louder," came the answer. "I didn't think I had it in me. In recollection, I must have looked like those cartoon women men are so fond of who leap onto a chair and scream their heads off when they see a mouse."

"What I don't understand," Claire was intervening, "is how he could sort of sit there, if you see what I mean, with a knife in his back, without your seeing it. He must have been leaning forward a bit. I mean, he couldn't be leaning backward, could he? The knife would have got in the way. Well, wouldn't it?"

"Ugh! You're making me nauseated." This from Emma.

"I'd have asked that question if you hadn't." Victor seemed to agree with his elder daughter.

"Believe me, the *commissaire* thought of that too. But, you know the back seat in a French bus curves round to the side, so, although we were sitting beside each other, he was really at right angles to me and there was no way I could see his back. Besides, there was nobody else on the back seat, so we weren't actually touching or anything."

"And he just lolled there?" Claire clearly found the details enthralling.

"Yes. You know the buses in Paris are always lurching round corners or pulling out around traffic, so it seemed fairly normal to me that he should be swaying a lot. In any case, most of the time I wasn't really thinking about anything. First of all, I was reading. Secondly, you only look for explanations when you know one is necessary. I just thought he was sleeping."

Sara paused for a while then added: "Actually, the hilt wasn't very big at all. In fact, it was remarkably short, now I come to think about it. Also, it was very dark, so it wouldn't have shown up very well against his suit. It's just that when he fell on me," she shuddered, "it was obvious, because it had the light on it and because I was staring down at him."

"But the blade must have been humungous," said Emma, beginning to take an interest in the ramifications of the story. "There was no blood, you say, so the knife must have penetrated his heart. At least, that's what they say in all the books and movies."

"I believe so. Perhaps the knife was specially made or altered in some way. The French police were certainly surprised by its shape; they told me that, without specifying why. But that's enough. I really don't want to discuss it any more tonight. What's the news on the home front?"

First came the domestic news. Claire's live-in boyfriend, David, a painter, had an exhibition coming up in a few days, his first for two years, and was working very hard to get everything ready. He had recently changed galleries and was pinning his hopes on his new dealer, his sister's "significant other," who had the reputation of really putting herself out for the artists in her stable. Emma's husband, Sacha, a college teacher, was away at a conference, but was otherwise well and happy, having recently completed the manuscript of a book about black holes, of which he boasted that it would never make the best-seller list.

All four grandchildren were away at the same summer camp for two weeks, learning to ride ponies, but were all due back on Saturday. Each daughter had two, a girl and a boy each, Marguerite and Patrice for Claire, seven going on eight and six; Suzanne and Daniel for Emma, seven and five and a half. The cousins made good company for each other. Sara made the proper grandmotherly noises and volunteered to find something exciting for them to do in the days following their return, providing the good weather held.

Politics and economics dominated the rest of the conversation. Another scandal was affecting the governing party in Quebec; inflation had taken off again; Ottawa was not alone in threatening another new, revised law that jeopardized women's rights. Demographic issues were rearing their ugly head. Sara was particularly depressed at the possibility of having to take to the streets to demonstrate yet again. Surely at her age, she was entitled to retire from active militancy. Alas, at home or abroad, it seemed as if every gain was constantly being menaced, for blacks, women, immigrants, all visible minorities, first nations, oppressed groups seeking independence, freethinkers, any mixture of the above. It was unending, like continuous motion. Worst of all was the apparent imminent demise of any attempt by people of different origin, sex, you name it, actually to live together in moderate harmony. It was becoming more important to be different than to assert your membership in the human race.

Victor announced that the City of Montreal was talking once more about raising taxes, and rumblings from the public transport employees seemed to suggest that they might be thinking in terms of reviving one of their more unpleasant traditions, happily dormant over the previous few years, an annual bus and metro strike.

At that point the telephone rang. David wished to welcome Sara back and apologized for not being able to do so in person. He was frantically mounting canvases and had absolutely no time to spare. His mother-in-fact if not in-law made reassuring sounds and promised to bring all sorts of interesting people to the opening in the hope that some of them would buy. She had scarcely put the phone down than another call came through, from a close friend of hers with a problem she wished to discuss and who had obviously been counting the days till her return. Sara promised to call back the following morning to arrange an appointment, put the phone down, turned on the answering machine to get some respite and made her way back to the table.

Paris was seeming more and more remote.

"Is there no good news?" Sara asked plaintively. "Friends with problems, taxes, rising unemployment no doubt. Much more of this and I shall have to head for a nursing home."

"I don't know about good news," her husband said, "but there is something that in the excitement I forgot to tell you. You got a call yesterday from a Staff-Sergeant Bernard. R.C.M.P., I think. He'll get in touch with you tomorrow after you've recovered from your jet lag."

Sara choked over her wine.

CHAPTER FIVE

The Montreal Connection

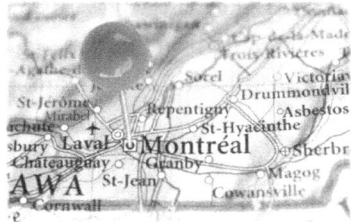

Staff-Sergeant Bernard was not alone when he called at Sara's house the following afternoon.

His promised phone call had come rather early in the day, and it was only because of her jet lag that Sara had been up at all. It always took her several days to recover from the time change. Unlike most of the people she spoke to, it was more difficult for her to fly from east to west than in the other direction, possibly because she preferred going the other way.

Four a.m. had, therefore, seen her up with the all too noisy birds, and she was certainly about, if not exactly alert and intelligent, by the time the phone rang. She had by then slipped downstairs quietly in order not to disturb Victor and taken her breakfast on the back deck. Afterwards, she made a few unsuccessful friendly overtures to the cats, skimmed several literary magazines that had been awaiting her return, flipped through the interesting looking letters in her pile of mail, tossed her bills into what she called her "see-you-later" pile and finally reminded her husband that he had to get up to go to work.

She was in fact relaxing on a chaise longue when the strident ringing interrupted her reverie, provoking in her the customary panic that one of her daughters was calling with bad news. A pleasant male voice greeted her, however, identifying itself as coming from Staff-Sergeant Bernard and asking if he might drop by to see her, almost as if it were a neighbourly visit.

Pleased as she was, as a taxpayer, to see the R.C.M.P. starting the day betimes, as it were, it nevertheless seemed to her that seven-thirty a.m. was an unreasonable hour to expect anyone actually to answer the telephone. With the possible exception, of course, of the hosts of early morning talk shows. It was irritation then, or pig-headedness rather than a long list of previous engagements, that caused her to postpone until the afternoon the appointment Staff-Sergeant Bernard was so politely asking for.

Later, as the hours ticked away with unbearable slowness and she found herself unable to concentrate on any of her most normal activities because of the curiosity that was eating her up, Sara was to regret not having invited him over on the spot. She spoke curtly to Victor as he headed out the door, harangued the mailman for failing to notice the Do Not Fold sticker on one of the envelopes he was delivering, used the wrong cycle for her delicate washing, broke a cup and let the milk she was heating in the kitchen for her eleven o'clock *café crème* boil over.

"You're not even half listening," complained her friend, Edna, over lunch at the *café Laurier* where the two had agreed to meet when they spoke earlier in the day. Situated on trendy Laurier Avenue in Outremont, it was a favourite haunt of the French-speaking chic bourgeoisie, and both Emma and Sara loved the continental atmosphere. "When we spoke last night, I told you I had a problem to discuss. That's why we agreed to meet here for lunch, and now you haven't heard a word I said. You probably haven't even noticed what you're eating."

"Yes, I have. Carrot *soufflé*. Never suggest I don't know what's on my plate. You know how I enjoy my food! I'm truly sorry to appear a little absentminded, there are problems on my mind too, but you were saying that your husband's about to go on sabbatical leave from his university and you're not happy."

Edna nodded, her bright blue eyes staring a little pathetically at Sara from beneath the thick lock of shiny black hair artistically arranged over her brow. "Well, for his research, you know he's working on the history of Canadian travellers in West Africa, missionaries and things, he needs to spend most of his year in Senegal and Paris. No, don't laugh. Of course, it's great, and normally who wouldn't want to spend time in Saint-Louis or Dakar, let alone France..."

"But...? Come on, Edna, what's the but?"

"I just don't want to. In one way, it would be terrific, particularly now the children are grown up and gone. But you know what translation's like. It's taken me quite a few years to build up my contacts to the point where I can earn a good living without working for an agency. Of course, with the Internet, I could probably still continue freelancing over there, but it's important for me to keep that personal touch. If I disappear now for a year or even six months, I might lose some contacts and even contracts. Who knows whether I'll get any local work. I could end up back to square one. And, apart from that, I miss Montreal when I'm away from it for too long."

"I must admit," said Sara, "that the idea of working for an agency again, nine to five, churning out a set number of words a day for a mere pittance, holds no charm. What are your options? You could just stay here, couldn't you?"

"But apart from all other considerations, like whether we'll miss each other if we're apart for a year, that's expensive. On his earlier leaves, when the kids were small and I didn't take my career as seriously, we rented out the house in Montreal and that covered the cost of the place we took over in France or whatever. If I stay here, we can't do that, so Roland will have to fork out quite a lot of money, and he doesn't get a full salary on leave anyway."

"Well, with e-mail and faxes and computers, it might just be easier than you think to carry on working in Dakar or downtown Paris. You should look into that, although I agree that personal contact is very important when you're trying to pull off a deal. You must have some jobs on the go. Why not rent out your house as planned, take off with Roland for a month or two and finish off those translations? Then you can come back and stay with us for a couple of weeks while you look around for more."

"You know that's worth thinking about. I feel a lot better now," Edna replied. "I can't really afford to flip constantly backwards and forwards across the Atlantic but I'll work on your idea. And thanks for the invitation. But there's also my mama to stay with, as long as she doesn't go on too much about how dangerous it is to leave any man alone for any length of time! Really, I think all these "traditional" women trust men less than we do. I'd be insulted if I were a man."

"There's only one miracle solution to your problem. We should both have become academics, married academic husbands and had academic leaves together. There's a frightening thought for you!"

Edna laughed briefly at her friend's sally before returning to her main preoccupation. During the rest of the meal, Sara continued outwardly to manifest sympathy while inwardly examining all the possible reasons for Staff-Sergeant Bernard's interest. Finally, as they were about to part, with no perfect solution in sight to Edna's problem, Sara, turning on the ignition of her car, heard her friend enquire about what had been troubling her.

"Appointment with a nice R.C.M.P. man," she cried, dashing off. "Call you tomorrow to tell all." Edna gazed in stupefaction after the little green Renault as it whizzed around the corner, bearing its owner away to her mysterious rendezvous. Sara, looking in the rear-view mirror and seeing her friend standing in the middle of the sidewalk with her mouth open, felt a glow of satisfaction at producing such an effect but also a little guilty. Never mind! Edna would get the full story before long. The glow subsided somewhat as she approached her house and had to steel herself for what might well be an ordeal.

At three p.m. the bell rang. Sara, desperately trying to look natural, as if visits from the police were everyday occurrences in her life, opened her door to find two people, a man and a woman, standing on her doorstep.

"Mrs. Thomas?" asked the man.

Who else is he expecting, Sara thought irritatedly, as she nodded her head in agreement that she was indeed who she was.

"Perhaps I should perform some introductions." The woman had stepped forward. "I am Sergeant Soraya Danesh of the *Sûreté du Québec,* the Quebec provincial police, and this is my colleague, Staff-Sergeant Simon Bernard, of the R.C.M.P. May we come in, please?"

Sara stepped back to let them through the door then ushered them into the dining room, on the principle that the table might make it easier for them to take notes. Her offer of coffee was accepted. Somehow that fact, plus the familiar fiddling with her espresso machine and setting out the cups and sugar, helped her over the first few minutes and enabled her to face her questioners with greater equanimity than she had expected.

They did not seem particularly frightening. Danesh, clearly bouncy and dynamic by nature, and of Iranian origin judging by her name, was obviously quite young, still well shy of thirty. That was normal, thought Sara, as police forces in Quebec had only recently made a drive to recruit women. Bernard, apparently less of an extrovert than his companion, probably in his early fifties, balding and a little overweight, was cultivating the fatherly or avuncular look. No doubt, concluded Sara, to lull criminals into a false sense of security and thereby encourage confessions.

"You must have guessed, Mrs. Thomas, that we are both here because of the murder you were involved in," he said, in the pleasant voice that went so well with the image he was projecting, and which rather contradicted the slight face he pulled as he tasted the bitter coffee.

"Hardly involved," came the answer. "I was an innocent bystander, you realize? I assume, by the way, you are referring to that poor Mr. Fainsilber and not trying to frame me for some other totally unrelated crime."

"We do not try to frame anyone," said Staff-Sergeant Bernard stiffly. His sense of humour obviously needed working on. "But yes, we are talking about Mr. Fainsilber. It appears he had links with Quebec; in fact he visited here very recently. He then flew directly to Israel where he remained only a short while before returning to Paris, where he was killed a few days later."

"Well, that hardly makes links." Sara emphasized the last word. "He could be simply a world traveller. No, you're right. If he was a Hassidic Jew, then he wouldn't just be trotting about all over the place. Every journey would have a reason."

"The reason is one of the things we are trying to

discover," Danesh chimed in, very perkily. "We were wondering, therefore, if you could help us with that."

"Not again! I told the *commissaire* Santal and the *juge d'instruction* everything I know and, believe me, it doesn't amount to much. But what I don't understand is why you're involved. If the murder was committed in Paris, surely the French police should be in charge of the investigation."

"As indeed they are. But they have asked for our cooperation in getting information, partly about his trip here and partly about you, and we have, of course, provided them with all we know -- and that doesn't amount to much either," his sense of humour was progressing. "We thought we would kill two birds with one stone, if you'll excuse the expression, by asking you if by any chance you knew something helpful."

"Nothing, I'm afraid. But, if it's only a routine information check, isn't it unusual for both the R.C.M.P. and the *Sûreté du Québec* to be working on the case?"

"Perhaps I can explain the procedure to you. I understand you translate detective stories so you may find what I am about to say useful." My goodness, Bernard was now smiling. "Because of the Montreal connection, France made a request for info. to Interpol..."

"Interpol! I knew this would turn out to be romantic," Sara breathed ecstatically. "Except, naturally, for the victim," she added hastily. "But it does sound like a Hitchcock movie, you must admit."

Danesh laughed. "It's more messy than romantic when you're on the working end, but I know what you mean. I loved The Thirty-Nine Steps. Saw it in a repertory theatre in Teheran when I was but a teenager before my family chose to leave and emigrate to Canada. Gave me a taste for mysteries. Perhaps, now I think of it, that's why I joined the police."

"Anyway," Bernard ploughed determinedly on, "Interpol spoke to the R.C.M.P. liaison officer in Paris who passed the request on to our headquarters here. Our superintendent opened a file and, as usual, passed it on to me. Normally, I would have asked my subordinates to pursue the matter, but there are a couple of aspects to the case that made the superintendent think I should hang on to the reins for the moment, but not for too long, I trust."

"Only he's asked me for help," added Danesh. "At least, he asked the *Sûreté*, and I got chosen. We like to cooperate whenever possible, particularly when there's overlapping jurisdiction."

"I'm still confused," murmured Sara, whose head was beginning to spin ever so slightly. "What overlapping jurisdiction?"

"Well," Danesh responded, "whenever someone who travels a great deal, particularly to or from the Middle East, is murdered, we think drugs. The *Sûreté* is always interested in pursuing that little avenue, especially if Quebec is in any way involved, even though the import/export end of it really belongs to the Mounties. But the R.C.M.P. also has another trail to follow, so they decided, and we agreed, that we should join forces, if you'll excuse the pun."

"But why not the *Service de Police de la Ville de Montréal* police? I live in Montreal, after all."

"They are informed, naturally, of our activities. But

Rabbi Fainsilber, or the would-be rabbi Fainsilber, had connections outside the Greater Montreal area, and that's also our jurisdiction. We are the only police force for most of Quebec. Besides, when it comes to drugs, the Montreal *Service de Police* drug squad does not necessarily have the means that we have."

"Can you tell me what the other trail is? If I'm not a serious suspect, that is?"

This time, Staff-Sergeant Bernard answered. "A list was found in one of the books he was carrying. In his recent travels, the deceased is known to have had contacts with Nazi-hunters, those who track down war criminals. You know another enquiry is currently taking place in Canada about such persons, who were given or somehow obtained Canadian citizenship and have been living here for many years without ever being harassed or paying the price for their crimes. Well, our superiors hypothesize, although we don't necessarily agree, that the names on the list may just be the aliases of war criminals that our victim intended to turn over."

"I knew it, I knew it." Sara was quite excited. "I knew that list was important even though the *commissaire* dismissed it. Of course, the people would have to be pretty old by now, but still... Can I see it?"

"That scarcely seems appropriate." Danesh's reluctance was obvious, and Bernard apparently shared her reticence.

"Nonsense. Maybe I'll know some of them and can give you some information. If not, what does it matter? I'm not going to photocopy it."

She had a photographic memory but was not about to

tell her interviewers so.

The two police agents consulted each other silently and fell in with her suggestion, both nodding their heads. The list was produced, and Sara scanned it very carefully. There were seven names all told.

"Are these the people's real names or their pseudonyms?" she asked.

"If we knew that, we'd know everything," said Danesh.

"Well, how do you know these are criminals hiding in Canada, rather than in Uruguay or, I don't know, South Africa? How do you know they're criminals at all?"

"We don't. We don't know anything. But, given the fact that, outside Israel, Canada's the only country he's visited, apart from France where he lived, I think it's unlikely we have to worry about Latin America or Africa. Of course, the list could just be the names of people he wanted to invite to a Bat or Bar Mitzvah, for all we know. It bears looking into, though, you must admit."

Sara admitted.

"And let's not forget," added Bernard, "they could be dope dealers just as easily as war criminals. Fainsilber wouldn't be the first to hide behind a religious appearance to commit dastardly deeds. There are precedents in Montreal even."

Sara was irresistibly reminded of her dinner in Paris and her friend Hélène's jesting remarks about no one stopping a rabbi to look for drugs. Truth and fiction were turning out to be very similar, at least potentially.

"So, do these names mean anything to you?" Bernard was curious.

She wondered whether he thought it was war criminals or drug dealers that she frequented. "No, I don't recognize a single one. Sorry." And she truly was. The case was really beginning to interest her and not just because she was "involved."

Up to that point, she had been indifferent rather than anything else to the outcome, even if, as a good citizen, she hoped the murderer would be caught. Her main concern, though, apart from the bad dreams that had disturbed her sleep several nights in a row, had been convincing first the French then the Canadian police that she was completely innocent.

Now that they seemed satisfied that she had indeed had nothing to do with the corpse in the bus, her temporary neighbour, as someone had said, perhaps herself, she should have felt completely disengaged. It was not, after all, her responsibility to see the assassin brought to justice. But she knew she would miss the stimulation of being close to the centre of the enquiry.

That was not her main reason, however, for not wanting to be shut out. The mere mention of war-criminals had been like a red rag to a bull, if that is an appropriate simile for a woman. Sara had, since her childhood, been repelled and fascinated by the story of the Holocaust, had read books, viewed fiction and documentary films on the topic, been disgusted by the welcome known war criminals had received in many countries. She had followed all the cases involving former Nazis and neo-Nazis at home and abroad.

Her interest was not prurient. It seemed to her that

understanding the mentality that underlay the Nazi apparatus for extermination, as also, possibly to a different degree, apartheid, was essential if humans were to make any progress at all towards a common humanity, an ideal that seemed to be vanishing from view all too rapidly.

Staff-Sergeant Bernard was still speaking, but it was only with an effort that Sara managed to focus her attention once again on what he was saying. She knew she had missed part of it, but, if the end was anything to judge by, he was merely mouthing polite platitudes in order to wind down the interview in the most courteous manner possible. Danesh was clearly preparing to go through the same exercise.

"Please," said Sara, "is there any way in which I can be kept informed of your progress? I am really very interested in the possibilities you outline, and I am sort of involved." This from someone who had denied any involvement earlier in the meeting.

"It is not our custom," responded Bernard stiffly, "apart from our normal press conferences, to keep the general public informed of our activities, particularly when an enquiry is not yet finished."

Sara remembered that once, many years before, her car had been stolen. The police had returned it, but no-one had ever bothered to tell her what had happened to the car-thief, even when the enquiry was over. A very unsatisfactory arrangement. Should there not be someone in charge of follow-ups?

Her displeasure must have shown on her face, because Danesh picked up after he had finished, smiling.

"Perhaps, if you phone me now and then, I shall be able to give you some information. Nothing confidential, of course, but I understand that it would be very frustrating for you to feel completely shut out. We'll do what we can. It may not be much, but perhaps better than nothing."

As she ushered the two police agents out of her house, although inwardly seething, Sara tried very hard to look pleased at being thrown this mini-bone. It was an unknown and innocent child, going from door to door to collect money for a marathon, or a school play or some charitable organization or other who bore the full brunt of Sara's unseeing angry glare as the police car drove away down the street, its occupants blissfully unaware, as indeed she was for the moment, that a secret resolve was crystallizing in her subconscious mind.

"Nothing confidential, of course... Perhaps better than nothing," she mimicked through gritted teeth, almost knocking over the hapless child collector on the doorstep, as she mindlessly slammed the door in his face. She grabbed a pad and pen and began writing down the names on the list they had shown her. Five, six, seven, that was it. Seven names, all told. She looked at them again, but they were still unfamiliar. If only, she thought, if only...

The sound of the telephone ringing interrupted her reverie.

"C'est toi, Sara? This is Huguette. Did you have a good trip?" The speaker swept on without waiting for an answer. "Listen, I'm going to be in your neighbourhood this evening. Business. House business. Can I drop in for a coffee? About nine-thirty? Should be through by then."

Sara barely had time to say she'd be delighted, before the voice continued.

"I'm so looking forward to seeing you again after all this time. It's been absolutely ages, and so many things have happened, to both of us, I expect. We'll have a good natter, about your plans and mine. Make arrangements to spend more time together. Anyway, it's too bad, can't chat now. In a tremendous rush. See you later. Love to Victor ..."

The last few words were followed by a mumble. Sara was mildly intrigued. Huguette Verdon, an old friend, was a lawyer, and those who knew her well used to say that she won her cases because the opposition never got a chance to speak. It was unlike her to be inaudible. Ah well. All would no doubt become clear that evening. Sara picked up her purse and a few other belongings before going upstairs to her study to clear away some of the accumulated work piled up on her desk.

Suddenly she stopped in her tracks as her internal ear finally made sense of her friend's last words. Could Huguette possibly have said: "Have to talk to you about a murder?"

CHAPTER SIX

The Long Arm

When Victor arrived home after work that evening, he found his wife mulling over a translation problem. So deeply immersed was she that it was only after he had stomped up the stairs and coughed like a consumptive at the door of her study, that Sara realized anyone was in the house.

"This piece isn't difficult to translate," she explained, raising her head from her work, "once you've made certain decisions about the style. It's just that it's not quite clear what I could or should get away with in French."

She was sitting at an unexpectedly modern piece of furniture of Scandinavian design. While Sara had chosen to furnish the rest of her house in a more traditional style suited to its venerable age, she preferred her workspace to have the clean lines that suggest efficiency and practicality.

The desk she had chosen combined a workstation for her computer and printer with a large surface for her to spread her papers and dictionaries about while she worked. Bookshelves lined three of the walls. There she kept only copies of the books and articles she had translated along with her specialized dictionaries and reference materials. A large bow window on the fourth wall provided plenty of natural light during the day and allowed her to gaze at the small park across the street and listen in fine weather to the sounds of children playing.

Victor was no translator but, after more than thirty years of marriage with Sara, he was sufficiently acquainted with the basic vocabulary and issues to be able to nod or shake his head comprehendingly in all the right places whether he understood or not what she was chuntering about. This situation clearly called for a sympathetic nod.

"You see, the style in Canadian English is, to put it mildly, laconic. The effect is based on repetition and minimality. Does that word exist, by the way? Remind me to look it up. Anyway, what makes an impact in English just looks badly written in French, as if Camus had never got past grade 2. So really, I have to decide what constitutes acceptable minimality in French, I suppose, here and in France. God, I dread the thought of having to read any more minimalist writing, however fashionable it may be. It all just makes me yearn for Balzac or George Sand."

Victor forbore to ask why she did not settle for a literal translation. They had been through that discussion many times before. He well knew Sara was on the side of those who believed in interpreting and reconstituting meaning rather than those who wanted you to read a translation as if it were just that, a translation. Sometimes he thought his life would have been easier if she had belonged to the second group. But less interesting, certainly, he added hastily to himself, not wanting to appear disloyal even in thought. He offered to pour a drink while she thought about the question.

"Give me a *pastis*, a light one," she begged. "I'll be finished in a minute. Oh, and I made some anchovy butter and left it in the refrigerator. Spread some on a couple of *canapés*, at the same time, there's a love. We'll make believe we're sitting sipping our drinks on a terrace in the shade of some plane trees in the south of France on a hill overlooking the Mediterranean."

"You're on," said Victor. "Consider it a rehearsal for our golden years. I see us declining slowly and pleasantly in the sun and warmth of the Riviera, with an annual summer trip back to Montreal to keep in touch with the girls and old friends. Way to go! In the meantime, you can also meditate on what we're to eat tonight. I see you didn't buy anything, and neither did I."

They sipped their drinks on the large back deck that Victor had built when they installed in their dining room French doors leading out to the garden. Neither had ever understood why so few of the older houses had easy access to the outside and had decided to remedy the situation as far as their own was concerned. Victor had also built a kind of frame over the deck over which he had trained a few grape vines, creating a shady arbour they particularly appreciated.

As they sat, they admired Victor's tomatoes in his small

patch of vegetable garden and the quite splendid flowerbeds next door. It was all very peaceful, and, for a while, they could almost convince themselves they were sitting in a small square in a remote village in the *arrière-pays* or the back country behind Grasse or Villefranche.

At least they could until Sara found herself recounting her afternoon visit, a visit that brought home to Victor, almost for the first time, the reality of the experience she had undergone. Having the police in the house gave it a consistency that had hitherto been lacking. He felt, a little guiltily, that he had perhaps underestimated the impact on Sara of the gruesome discovery and its aftermath, let alone the long-buried memories it must arouse. It had all seemed so remote until then, rather like sepia scenes from a half-forgotten movie, but suddenly he felt as if he'd been plunged with insufficient warning into something X-rated in virulent technicolor or even some form of virtual reality.

It was with some relief then, that he learned that both the R.C.M.P. and the *Sûreté* had apparently given Sara a clean bill of health, and that there was no need for her to be further involved in this very upsetting enquiry. In his relief, he failed to hear the faint note of disappointment in her voice as she told him of their snub-like reaction to her curiosity. Without actually bending the truth, she in turn was careful not to tell him she had reconstituted the names on the would-be rabbi's list.

When they had finished discussing the case, a companionable silence reigned for a while, then Sara spoke, almost hesitantly.

"Darling, at the risk of sounding plebeian after the

drink and the smashing *canapés*, do you know what I'd truly like for dinner? I'd like us to send out for a pizza. That would be such a North American thing to do, don't you think? God, what a snob I sound, I don't mean to, but it would really prove I'm back, wouldn't it? Besides, to tell the awful truth, I actually prefer Montreal pizzas to the ones they serve in Paris."

Victor burst out laughing.

"My gourmet wife. Of course. It's a good idea. We'll order a huge pizza all-dressed, eat it in front of the television set and wash it down with a bottle of Italian wine. You don't mind if I draw the line at beer, do you? I really don't feel like any tonight. And, for dessert, there's a good movie on later this evening if you're at all interested. An old Frank Capra."

"Sorry, darling. I'll have to pass if you don't mind too much. Huguette is coming over at nine-thirty or thereabouts. You watch the movie; you don't have to bother about us. We'll have a cup of coffee in the kitchen or upstairs. Believe me, she'll still be here when the movie's over. We can all have a brandy or something, and you can have a chat with her then. O.K.? It'll do me good to stay up late, help me sleep past the dawn chorus tomorrow morning."

Victor nodded his acquiescence and pottered off to call the local pizza parlour, while Sara, in the kitchen, busied herself with washing the lettuce and preparing the vinaigrette for the salad they would eat with it.

"You know," she added, a little diffidently, when Victor had finished, "I could swear that Huguette said she wanted to discuss a murder with me. It was difficult to make out what she was saying at the end, she must have turned away from the telephone because someone at the office was speaking to her, but when I thought about it, that's what it sounded like. Can it be possible? Am I hallucinating?"

"You don't think that, instead of putting it behind you, you're letting yourself become obsessed with what happened in Paris, do you?" came the response. "She could have been saying 'merger' or 'muddle'; all sorts of possibilities come to mind. And if, as you say, Huguette wasn't really speaking into the phone, she could even have been responding to something that had been said by whoever was standing beside her, which makes 'merger' even more likely."

"You're quite right. And even if you aren't, we'll find out soon enough. Come on. Let's set everything out so we're ready when the pizza arrives. Can't bear it cold. I put some pesto in the salad dressing, by the way. I know you like that."

When Huguette rang the doorbell later that evening, Victor was already sitting in front of the television set, engrossed in the opening scenes of *Mr. Smith Goes to Washington*, and Sara was back at her desk, fighting more with her jet lag than with her translation. Her brain was completely foggy, and the arrival of her friend was just what she needed to jog her into wakefulness.

The two women embraced and, after making coffee, decided to drink it in the upstairs study so as not to disturb Victor's concentration on the film. Although they spoke occasionally on the phone, they had not seen each other for nearly a year, so they had a great deal to catch up on.

Huguette, a tall brunette, a little on the plump side, was a childless *divorcée* in her late-forties. Apart from news of their respective careers, one had to catch up on anecdotes about daughters and grandchildren, the other had to listen to stories about various friends and holidays at tropical resorts.

"What's the house business that brings you to this neighbourhood?" Sara asked finally. "Are you branching out into real estate?"

"That could be truer than you think but more of that later or maybe another day. No, after all these years, I've decided to become the proud owner of a house."

"A house! But you live in that splendid apartment in Old Montreal. Everybody adores it. You must be mad."

"That's what I'd have thought a few months ago, as you well know, but my landlord, whom I shall refrain from describing, in order to protect your dainty ears, has finally decided to turn the building into condos."

Sara gasped.

"That's illegal, isn't it?" she exclaimed.

"You're talking to a lawyer, don't forget," said Huguette with some bitterness. "Of course it's not illegal any more in our progressive society, and in any case, bit by bit, all the other tenants have moved out, I don't know why. Bought off, maybe. Or scared off, for all I know. There are only two of us left. Naturally we can hang on and make it impossible for him to go ahead. But equally naturally, he can make our lives extremely difficult."

"Can't you fight him?"

"Of course, I can. But I feel that it's not worth it. Don't

tell me it's a cop out, I know that. But I'm not getting any younger. And suddenly, the thought of fighting yet another battle fails to appeal."

It was certainly true that Huguette had spent most of her life fighting battles of one kind or another, usually involving principles and other people's wrongs. As a lawyer, she tended to attract more than her fair share of immigration or spousal abuse cases, and she was certainly no stranger to pro bono cases, hardly charging for pencils in her pursuit of justice. That was why she had never reached the income level of some of her less qualified colleagues who had always taken on only those propositions that were particularly remunerative. "Virtue is still its own reward," thought Sara. "You certainly don't get anything else."

"Besides," Huguette continued, "the idea of becoming a property owner in my old age has its charms, and, if I'm going to join the Establishment, I don't feel like doing it with a condo. You spend half your life trying to convince a bunch of reticent co-owners that the awning you want to put up will enhance the building and the other half trying to earn enough money to pay your share of what some other people have decided to install and that you don't like. No, it's a house for me, even if you have to do your own worrying about getting the lawn mowed and the plumbing fixed. So, I've been visiting one on your street."

"Charles and Vera," gasped Sara. "Oh, how perfect that would be. You know the people who put it up for sale are old friends of ours; you must have met them; they've been at all our parties. Anyway, they've retired to the South of France apparently, and I was rather depressed at the thought of seeing strangers in there. I'm so used to just dropping in that I had visions of myself doing just that one day in a fit of absent-mindedness and either frightening the new owners to death or ending up in a prison cell for illegal entry!"

"Or both," commented Huguette with her attractive crooked smile. "Well, we'll see how it goes. It's certainly very appealing, and being close to you would be a plus, but the price will have to come down a bit. Also, and this is the news I've been saving till last, it's just possible that someone will be moving in with me. Curiously enough, he's actually more enthusiastic about buying that particular house than I am and convinced me to put a bid in. But, as I mentioned, the price will have to come down. Certainly our bid is much lower than the asking price so God knows whether they'll accept."

Sara was suitably surprised. "You told me over the phone just before I left you had a new love interest, but you didn't say it was serious. Things have moved on since we last spoke. Moving in together. Buying a house together. That makes it pretty permanent. It sounds almost like a second marriage. Should I start saving up for a present? Housewarming or wedding?"

"Not either straightaway, you old matchmaker. It's all a bit up in the air. As I mentioned, we've only known each other a few weeks, two or three months maybe, but we get along well, like the same movies, the same music."

"You must have discovered all that very quickly. I'm impressed by your speed. Or by his!"

"A bit of both. You know, at my age, one doesn't need

a two-year engagement. On the other hand, one doesn't want to be too precipitate. Once bitten, *n'est-ce pas*? I think you'll find him simpatico. He's very urbane. Travels a lot. He was in Germany recently. In fact, he's just come back."

In response to Sara's question about whose idea it had been that they share living quarters, Huguette said it had all been Richard's initiative, Richard being the friend under discussion. "His apartment's even fancier than mine but he's tired of rabbit hutch living, or so he says. Perhaps as we get older, we all have visions of homes covered with honeysuckle and warm odours of baking."

"That'll be a frosty Friday," Sara riposted, "the day your home is filled with warm odours of baking. I always think of you as the queen of frozen food."

"But always gourmet!" Huguette laughed as she responded to Sara's image of her. "In fact," she added, "visions apart, he seemed particularly keen on this neighbourhood. He's the one who saw the For Sale sign and suggested I suss out the house. I'd already told him you lived on this street and are one of my closest friends, so that probably weighed somewhat in the balance. What's more, now I come to think of it, it was Richard who thought of my dropping in here tonight. And not just because of the murder, either."

Sara's reaction was rather slow. When she thought about it later, she hoped it was just the jet lag. Just as she was about to make some remark about Richard's kindness in thinking of her, a woman he'd never met, the meaning of Huguette's last sentence struck her. "Not because of the murder. What can you mean?" she gasped.

"Oh, didn't anyone tell you? Well, I suppose in Paris they didn't know, and, in any case, who would necessarily link you to me? Silly of me to assume it really…"

Sara interrupted her friend, her voice sharp with impatience. "For goodness' sake, explain what you're going on about instead of rambling on like that. You're driving me mad. All the stress has been bad enough without you adding to it with your elucubrations, your incomprehensible maundering."

"Do forgive me," said Huguette penitently. "You're quite right to be annoyed. Here it is in a nutshell. The murdered man who was sitting beside you on the bus in Paris, well, you know what I mean, is someone I've met."

"Good Heavens!" Sara was stunned. "I can't believe it. You knew him. How could that be? He's hardly ever been out of France and I think you've hardly ever been there. And you're not really likely to visit a rabbinical school when you do. You're putting me on. You haven't really told the police this, have you? They'll start suspecting me all over again. All they need is a link between Fainsilber and me, no matter how tenuous. Tell me you're joking." She was clearly genuinely upset at the possibility. Huguette reached out a tentative hand to comfort her.

"You'll feel better when your jet lag has worn off. Just now you're tired out of your mind. I'm sorry to add more stress to what you've already been through. But, it's true. I knew him, and, yes, I've told the police, although they don't know you and I are friends. How would they ever find out? Besides, you don't really believe such a tenuous link would be important. It's the fatigue that's talking. Come on, don't be cross."

Sara shook her head in resignation and got up to go downstairs, saying she needed a drink, at least one and possibly two. Huguette followed her, continuing her explanation on the way down.

"The thing is I've been acting for a Hassidic community north of Montreal. The one that moved out of Outremont when they were left part ownership in all that land a few years ago. You must have read about it. There was quite a fuss in the papers. Some people in Outremont actually celebrated their departure! Remember? Yes, please." This to Sara who was waving a Scotch bottle at her.

"No ice, just a little water, as usual. Anyway, they hired our firm for some of their business deals, I have no idea why, since many of us are goyim, and no-one is Hassidic, of course; it all seems very strange to me, but the fact remains that I was designated to look after some of their affairs. Only speaking to the head honcho, naturally, who always keeps his eyes down when speaking to me, very disconcerting, although he's perfectly pleasant to talk to. The man who was killed visited them not so very long ago to discuss some business matter, who knows what, they never told me. I was asked to meet him off the airport bus and drive him up there. So I did. And that's the extent of my acquaintance with him. But the community asked me to explain the connection to the police."

"Is that the fellow you vaguely introduced me to the day I was hanging around the Berri bus station?" Victor appeared, holding out his empty brandy snifter for a refill. "Can't remember now what I was doing there, but I do recall your being with somebody rather young with long ringlets, well, ringlets anyway, and a big black hat. It's still a great movie, by the way. The Frank Capra I was watching," he explained to Huguette who had clearly and understandably not followed his sudden switch from ringlets to movies.

On hearing Huguette agree that it was one and the same person, Sara moaned gently and topped up her Scotch. Victor turned to her. "Don't worry, darling. No-one could turn that into an international conspiracy. We didn't even shake hands. Just nodded."

"Great." Sara sounded bitter. "A close friend and my husband know the man who was killed beside me in France, and the police are going to believe that I didn't know him and that the whole thing is coincidence. I'm beginning to have doubts myself! You'll end up by driving me to drink!"

CHAPTER SEVEN
Moles Galore

The dawn chorus presented no problem to Sara the following morning. Thanks to her late night and the extra whisky, she caught up with her jet lag and slept until her normal waking-up time, 7.30 a.m. All was not joy, as she also had a slight hangover from the previous night's excesses. Perhaps, she mused, it was just the stress of hearing Huguette's and indeed Victor's news about the rabbi. He, poor thing, was beginning to remind her of the Ancient Mariner's albatross with herself playing the role of the aged sailor.

Usually, on waking up, while Victor was busy in the bathroom, she would lie in bed for a while, chatting to the cats, easing herself into the morning. She was in the habit of half listening either to Daybreak, the CBC early morning show in English, or to its French counterpart, CBF Bonjour, on Radio-Canada, both happily free from commercials.

That day started out as no exception, except for her favourite felines, obviously still sulking. Stretching comfortably, she reached over to turn on the radio, just in time to hear an accented voice announcing another scorcher with 90% humidity. No encouragement there to get up and start rushing around. Slow motion was definitely called for.

Suddenly her attention was captured by the word Nazi. Damn, she had missed what whoever it was had been saying; it could have been something to do with the commission of enquiry. Of course, it could also have been something quite different. Announcing another new movie on the topic, more phony diaries or further revelations about seemingly respectable European personalities. New heroes even, like that Japanese diplomat, about whom the Israelis had known all along, had even honoured, without his name having surfaced anywhere else for decades. Another mystery.

Another tragedy too. Yet another Algerian intellectual gunned down by fundamentalists. And no-one was talking about all the women who, according to some of her friends, were still being shot, knifed, or terrorized on a daily basis, although in fewer numbers, a situation found in Canada even, as well as in countries where democracy was as yet unknown. No wonder some people didn't listen to the news.

So much for easing into the day. That was definitely an idea whose time had come and gone. Groaning slightly, she pulled herself out of bed and went downstairs to join Victor over breakfast. Neither of them was particularly talkative at that time of day. They managed, however, to grunt out a few words, before he returned to his morning reading and she anguished over what she could eat to metabolize her hangover. Not much later, as he got up to head for the office, looking as rumpled as always, in spite of having put on a suit just back from the cleaner's, Sara said in what she hoped was a casual tone: "Did you listen to Daybreak just now while you were in the bathroom?"

Victor turned around very sharply. "Yes, I did. And I heard the comments about the Nazis. Don't think I don't know what you're getting at. I can't tell you what to do, but I wish you would put an end to this obsession. You're a translator not some ridiculous P.I. in an American novel. You're not Miss Marple either. Let the police get on with their work and you get on with yours."

Sara, quite taken aback by her husband's sudden vehemence, opened her mouth to protest but he overrode what she was going to say.

"Apart from how ridiculous you'd look pretending to be a detective, you should give some thought to your safety, and to the safety of those about you. This is a murder, and there I have no doubt the detective novels are correct, the second one is always easier than the first." His voice softened. "I'd hate to lose you again so soon after your return from France. Just remember that we love you."

He leaned over, dropped a light kiss on her hair and went out to the hallway. She could hear him gathering up his keys, wallet and various other objects before letting himself out the front door to go to work. She sat stunned for a moment.

"He really must be worried," she thought, "to react like that. Perhaps he's right and I should just drop it all. Yes, that's best; I'll drop the whole thing. But I wonder all the same what they did say about Nazis. It must be something about the inquiry or he wouldn't have cared. Maybe I'll ask Edna if she heard anything. And there'll surely be a podcast."

And with that, having both taken and broken her good resolution in one and the same breath, she busied herself tidying up the kitchen with a view to taking a long warm bath before tackling her minimalist translation.

That was one of the advantages of working out of your own house. You could choose your hours. And you almost never needed to take the bus or the metro at rush hour. Some people she knew complained about the loneliness but, after raising two children, Sara quite enjoyed the peace and quiet that were often hers during the day. After all, she could go out if she wanted to. And she did have her courses to teach, so that provided contact not just with colleagues but also with young people.

She relaxed into her bath, a huge old-fashioned cast iron tub with claws that allowed her to stretch out voluptuously. She had been fully intending in her mind to run through the events of the previous few days and try to make some sense of them, but after a while found herself drifting off to sleep instead. Mindful of her mother's admonitions to her as a child: "Now, don't fall asleep in the bath, you know it's dangerous, you might drown," admonitions which she had herself repeated to her own children after swearing during her youth never to behave like her mother, she gave up on her dream of a long warm bath and decided to settle down to work. There was a lot to catch up on, a contract due almost any day.

With the ceiling fan whirring gently so as not to disturb her various piles of paper, Sara booted her computer and pulled towards her the book she was translating as well as the notes she had compiled to help her. She plodded on painstakingly although every so often she seemed to hear Victor's voice asking Huguette if she was talking about the man he'd met at the bus station or Huguette explaining how it was she knew the dead rabbi. Or was it Richard? No, definitely Huguette, but Richard was interested in the story so perhaps he was also involved in some way. Had Huguette said he was a lawyer too? Come to think of it, she hadn't had a chance to say very much about him because of Sara's reaction. She'd have to phone Huguette, apologize to her and show greater interest in her old friend's love life.

She turned back to her translation and managed to draft another few pages by lunch time. They would need reworking but at least there was some progress. She decided to go out for a stroll before eating, maybe pick up a newspaper, *La Presse* for instance, which was the one Victor never managed to bring home. Perhaps she'd drop by the little West Indian store to buy a couple of their patties. They were always delicious and it was easier than making something herself.

The sun was beating down quite hard and the humidity level was beginning to rise. Nevertheless, in spite of the fact that with every passing year she found the extremes of temperature harder and harder to bear, in her cool dress and straw hat, Sara managed to enjoy walking along the thoroughfare near her street.

She appreciated the little specialty shops and loved to

browse in the second-hand stores that had been springing up lately, although they boded ill for the economy. The neighbourhood was definitely changing. Gone forever were all those marvelous elderly Eastern European ladies who had fled first the Nazis then the Communists, who had seemed to speak about six languages each and just dripped with culture. The cafes that had catered to them were long gone too.

There were more recent arrivals from Eastern European countries but they were a very different kettle of fish. Very pleasant but less international, perhaps because of their communist upbringing. There were also many Asians, and numerous immigrants from all over the Arab world. It was rather exciting to find oneself in the middle of such diversity. And it made for interesting eating as well, she said to herself, as, after picking up her patties, she noticed two new restaurants that had opened, one advertising Thai cuisine and the other Korean.

As long as BLTs, bagels with cream cheese and lox, and fish'n chips remained available for the moments when she was seized by fits of nostalgia, she was all for a wide range of choices. And with that thought, she dropped a couple of coins into the outstretched grasp of a panhandler, a youngish man who looked as if he'd rather have been gainfully employed. But perhaps that was just a facial expression he kept in reserve to soften up warm-hearted middle-aged and up ladies.

Later, she washed her patties down with the inevitable cup of strong Ceylon tea, Earl Grey being something she reserved for the late afternoon. As she did so, Sara remembered she had promised to phone Edna and explain her remark about the nice R.C.M.P. man. Gosh, that expression was a throwback. Right back to the Vietnam War when she, still very young and all her friends of roughly the same age, had demonstrated against it and signed petitions and so forth. They were then convinced their phone lines were bugged and used to end every conversation with: "Don't forget to say good night to the nice R.C.M.P. man."

Had Edna been one of them? She thought so but, with all that water under the bridge, couldn't quite remember. Well, there was only one way to make sure, and that meant putting through the promised call. At that time of day she probably wouldn't be interrupting her, so, leaning back in her chair, she dialed the familiar number.

Edna, who had been waiting impatiently for the news, and indeed could confirm her youthful involvement in the peace movement, was gratifyingly agog with curiosity. She ooh'd and aah'd in all the right places, knew when to sympathize, when to express horror and shock, even when to encourage. Sara was the heroine of the day of her own soap opera, and, as her friend, Edna naturally felt she bathed in some of the reflected notoriety.

"Do you know what happened to a friend of mine?" she would say when her turn came -- as it would -- to narrate, a little self-importantly, her version of the events. "So exciting! She told me all about it herself, you know. In fact, she told me before she told anyone else, well, except her family, naturally." All in all, a very satisfying conversation for both of them.

Just as she was about to hang up, Sara heard the call

waiting signal; hurriedly she switched lines. It looked as if she wasn't going to get a lot of work done that afternoon. Her daughter Claire's voice came down the line; she wanted to know how the interview had gone with the Mountie.

"I was going to call last night," she added, "but really I was working on a story and didn't get home till late. And then I still had some writing to do." Sara assured Claire she had no need to apologize.

"I'm a big girl," she heard herself saying. "No chaperones needed." Claire laughed as her mother proceeded with her story, which was beginning to acquire a life of its own, as well as more and more embellishments with every telling.

"At work, we've been doing a little bit of investigative reporting of our own on the whole question of war criminals in Canada," Claire told her mother. "On a daily basis, we're pretty much confined to what is turning up at the inquiry, but we have masses of information that we can use afterwards to present a kind of documentary. Mind you, these people aren't getting any younger. One wonders how many can be left. Of course, some of them were probably still very young at the end of the war, there's no upper or lower age limit on that kind of viciousness, and if they live to a ripe old age, then there must still be some around. Let alone the ideas they may be instilling in younger generations who may not measure the full horror of the people they're dealing with. In any case, I for one would like to know how such criminals got in in the first place. And that remark goes for all the new criminals from the new wars like Rwanda or Central Africa."

"What kind of information have you unearthed?" Sara asked. "I told you that, thanks to this ridiculous photographic memory of mine, I was able to make a copy of the list the rabbi, or almost rabbi, was carrying when he was killed. It would be interesting to see if any of the names on it match any you have. It would satisfy some of my curiosity to find out."

Claire, brought up, like her sister Emma, to devour detective novels, was enthusiastic. "Hang on," she said. "I'm going to get Emma on the line, because I think she can help us too, even if what I'm going to ask isn't the most ethical thing in the world. We'll have ourselves a conference call."

Emma was busy so Sara and Claire chatted for a while until their third musketeer was free. Mainly they talked about the children, Marguerite and Patrice, with an occasional reference to Emma's son and daughter, Daniel and Suzanne. Their basic and totally objective conclusion was that the world had never seen four more intelligent, more beautiful, more charming children. Just as they settled that, Emma finally came on, and, after a few minutes, Claire was able to outline her idea.

"Mummy will never settle down until this mystery is solved. And maybe we can't do it all, but we can both help with the list of names. Yes, you too, Emma. First of all, I have all the stuff we've got but can't yet publish, if ever. Secondly, I can tap very easily into the morgues of all the major newspapers in Canada because so much stuff is online now. And even where it isn't, I can ask people to pull files for me. So, I'll take the list of names and, when I've got time, run them through everything we've got or anything I can pick up. That way for instance, we'll know if they're in any way suspect or if any of them ever made the headlines for any reason."

"But where do I come in?" asked Emma.

"Well, you've got access to credit ratings, haven't you? I mean, if anyone comes in and wants to buy on credit, don't you check them out? You know how it operates. And any credit rating bureau has all sorts of info. On everybody. Who you quarrel with, who your first boyfriend was, how much money you still owe on your university loan. They're like the Czars in 19th century Russia. Total information. So, how about it?"

Sara intervened to remind them that, as Claire herself had earlier pointed out, it wouldn't exactly be ethical for Emma to do that. Theoretically, she had to have a good reason for consulting people's credit ratings.

"Well, it is a good reason," said Emma, who had been reluctant to let herself be persuaded by her sister's arguments until her mother stepped in to prevent her. Childhood reactions don't always disappear overnight, after all.

"Besides, it's true that I'm always accessing people's credit. Not just for those buying on credit; even when I hire, I do that. And they certainly seem to know a lot, not all of it true unfortunately. Not long ago, I was chatting with a judge I met at a dinner-party and he was explaining that he was having a great deal of difficulty correcting his rating. He has the same name as a man with a very bad money record, the two of them had become mixed up somewhere in the innards of a computer, so the judge couldn't get a car loan!

Very funny, when you think of it. Of course, it may take him a long time but he's in a position to make sure it will get fixed someday. Pity the poor yobs who don't have his influence and who are stuck with other people's mistakes."

Sara was even more disturbed.

"But we're not going to use this stuff against any of these people," Claire argued. "We just want to find out if they exist and where, and also whether they were born here or not. Of course, genuine war criminals probably have completely false identities that prove their ancestors came over on the Canadian equivalent of the Mayflower; God knows that's easy enough in Canada, but it's worth a try. At least we'll have the impression we're doing something. Come on, say yes."

"How are David and Sacha going to react to all this?" her mother responded feebly, wondering simultaneously why she was suddenly talking like a nineteenth-century maiden instead of the strong independent woman she had thought she was. "Your father is not at all amused, I can tell you. We're treating it a bit like a game, but it really isn't one."

"Well, so far," this from Emma, "all we've agreed to is to consult some files in various offices, and that's quite a normal activity. How could anyone involved in the murder find out, unless by some freak of fate they work in a credit bureau or in a newspaper morgue? And you must admit, that would really be pushing coincidence a bit far. And what's it got to do with David and Sacha? I mean, I think we should probably tell them, but they can hardly crack the whip or lock us up in our rooms with a lot of yellow paper on the walls, like the poor woman in the Charlotte Perkins Gilman story."

Although she was not quite convinced that Emma was completely right about Gilman, Sara gave in and nervously dictated the names to her daughters over the phone, hoping that no-one else could overhear and, while doing so, recognizing her own incipient paranoia. Claire then promised to scan and e-mail her any reports, clippings and so on that she came across concerning the famous inquiry, so that her mother could bring herself up-to-date.

"I could probably also e-mail some of the videos I have of all our TV coverage." said Claire. "The new stuff we have I can't release yet, but you should have enough material to understand what's going on. That'll keep you busy while we're doing our research, and our darling father need never know what you're up to. Tell him you're starting up a press clipping agency. How's that?"

"Very funny," came the response. "Let's say I'll begin there, but I can't just sit still while you're doing all that work. You've given me some good ideas on how to set about getting information. There's a lot more of it lying around these days than there used to be, and we all have contacts that might prove useful. I'll keep you posted." And before her daughters could say another word, she promised not to attempt anything dangerous, although she didn't even know what that might be, and hung up.

The realization had just come to her that one of her good friends worked for a national Jewish organization. It might not be a bad idea to give him a call and ask to see him, either at his office or over a drink. For what she wanted, the office might be better. Five minutes later, she had an appointment for the following day. Peter had been somewhat bemused to be asked for a formal appointment without any reason being revealed; usually they met at parties or over dinner, but he was nevertheless quite content to make the arrangement, suggesting only that once their business was over they should have lunch together. Very civilized, she thought.

That evening over supper, Victor asked, rather pointedly, she concluded, how she had spent her day. Sara was able to reply quite truthfully that after a bout of translation and a stroll around the neighbourhood, she had chatted with her daughters about their children and reminisced with Edna about the war in Vietnam and the peace movement. It was a good thing the table was hiding her crossed fingers. Having had a tiring day trying to persuade a client it would be better if he came clean about his taxes, Victor failed to pick up on the hidden text in his wife's reply. That allowed them to spend the next few hours reading and watching television in perfect harmony.

CHAPTER EIGHT

What Are Friends For?

In many ways, as far as any investigation was concerned, the meeting with Peter, although agreeable, was a non-event. As she struggled up the hill toward his office, Sara admired once again, through the beads of sweat running down her face, the elegant modern architecture of the building, wishing only that the decision makers had seen fit to build it in one of the more level areas of Montreal.

Sara had never been able to understand why, in a city that sweltered in summer and had such incredibly long winters when the streets were covered in snow and ice, it was considered more up-market to live on a slope than on the flat. A death wish perhaps or a voluntarist attitude to ambient reality. Along the lines of 'I'm rich and there's nothing in nature that I can't overcome.' Sara was more modest and had chosen to live where she didn't need climbing boots and an alpenstock every time she left the house in winter. That also meant less effort to make when the sun was beating down.

As usual, habit rather than thought had unfortunately kicked in when she had gone to the bus stop. Instead of taking one that would have allowed her to walk down the hill, she had simply taken the direction she usually followed when heading off to teach her courses in somewhat the same area, albeit on a lower plane. That was why she was now panting up the hill instead, meditating once again on the vagaries of Montreal city-dwellers and their propensity for choosing difficulty.

Peter, short, fat and jolly looking, was already waiting for her in the entrance hall and he gently walked her along the carpeted corridor to his ground floor office. There, his furniture, also very modern, and rather Bauhaus in appearance given its very functionalist design, was overshadowed by a quite splendid abstract mural in which vivid colours dominated. Sara could almost feel them pulsing.

Apparently happy to see her, Peter thoughtfully gave his visitor a few minutes to recover from the heat and exertion before pressing unsweetened iced tea and cookies into her outstretched hand. They chatted for a while as a prelude to the serious part of the discussion. They covered some new art shows including Sara's pet hate, installations, his most recent trip to Israel, the snazzy restaurant a friend had just opened up near Sara's home, a new book on the history of the Communist Party in Quebec.

Eventually, however, the reason for her visit had to be

announced. Peter, who had read about the future rabbi's murder, had no idea of her role in the story. He seemed quite fascinated by her retelling of the recent events in her life and even tossed in the thought that, of course, many people she had come into contact with must have thought she herself was Jewish, given her first name. Rather than Protestant, he added, although he knew that no-one in her family had practiced a religion of any kind for several generations. Curious, this seemingly generalized need to identify people according to irrelevant categories. "And that," said Peter, still referring to her apparent Judaism, "might even have seemed all the more suspicious to your various police persons." She hadn't even thought of that possibility!

As for the names themselves, however, he was of little help. None of them, he declared, were familiar to him, and that probably meant they were not on any official list of people to be charged either with crimes against humanity or with hate-mongering. He was reluctant to start any enquiries about them because of the official nature of his position; questions coming from him might do serious harm to perfectly innocent people. But he did take a copy of the list and, locking it in his desk, promised to let her know if anything should transpire. And with that she had to be satisfied. For the time being.

In order to make it clear in the politest possible way that he did not wish to discuss the issue any further, he picked up the phone to call a cab, announcing that it was surely time for lunch. Sara barely had time to collect her thoughts before finding herself ushered out of the air-conditioned building into an equally air-conditioned taxi. Peter sat beside her and gave directions to the driver who had a variety of signs plastered over his cab inviting them to find Jesus before it was too late.

Over lunch, which they ate in a downtown pub, all fake beams and plastic wood, where the food was average but where they served a good locally brewed beer, Peter did give her more information about the Hassidic movement. He himself was a secular Jew. In fact, he had been brought up not to consider himself a Jew at all, since in his family's view the word's only connotation was necessarily religious and could not therefore apply to him or them. In retrospect, the Holocaust or Shoah had changed his position on that issue as it had for many other people.

The word "Hassidic" originally meant pious, he explained to Sara. The first movement reported dated back to nearly 200 years B.C. at least that was what he'd been told. Since then other groups had grown up, mainly in Eastern Europe, but had naturally scattered across the globe every time there was a pogrom or other attempt at extermination. They had very strict rules, all based on their concept of the Law. Their ideas about women were not exactly modern; adult women were encouraged to keep their hair about an inch long in order to be more comfortable under their wigs; that meant almost shaving their heads at regular intervals; they also had to keep their head covered; marriage and child-bearing were usually the only destiny available to women. No Hassidic Jew was encouraged to communicate with Goyim or even other Jews, on the contrary. They really believed in keeping themselves to themselves.

Sara was always delighted to acquire such information. She had visited Christian organizations with similar structures, although perhaps not quite so closed off from contact with outsiders. The Mennonites, for instance, and the Hutterites. There were others too. To know them was, in some ways, like moving through history, travelling in a time machine with stopovers, depending on the date on which the sect or movement was founded, or living in a series of freeze frames.

Most people, she thought, were tempted at some point by the idea of simply stopping history, and in Canada it looked as if more and more groups were achieving just that, forming their own little enclaves inside the wider world. Probably some First Nation Canadians or Americans were aiming to do the same thing, live outside the ever-faster ticking of the technological clock. Still others clearly wanted to choose their own paths within its context.

Peter's voice interrupted her reverie. He was apologizing; he had to abandon her for another appointment. Perhaps he hadn't even noticed she hadn't been listening for the past few minutes. She hoped not. Particularly as he was insisting on picking up the tab. Always the gentleman. She suggested he bring his wife to dinner over the weekend, he replied that he would ask his wife to call Sara, and on that note they parted. He to head back to his office and she to make for the delightfully cool university library for a little lexicological and other research.

The library itself was well organized and user-friendly. The new building in which it was housed, however, and which resembled nothing so much as a botched attempt by a child to build a mediaeval fortress with his or her Lego, was in her opinion a major eyesore on what was already an extremely unattractive street. It seemed unfortunate that the university in question had not applied its usual quite high creative standards to this annex.

She quickly found an available computer and so was able to fill the gaps in her lexical knowledge quite quickly. After her initial nervousness a few years earlier when confronted for the first time by all the new technology, she had consulted her students about the best way to use it. That was a domain in which they were far more skilled than most of their instructors. They had taken great pleasure in explaining everything to her in the simplest possible language. She had been honing her skills ever since.

When her search was over, she decided to have a quick look for information about credit rating bureaus so that she could talk to her daughters about them in a more informed way. She couldn't help feeling a little guilty about the use to which they were going to be put. Did the end justify the means? The computerized catalogue threw up references to one or two magazines she thought she might find useful. As she was scanning the monitor, she noticed a publication called Response, which, according to the catalogue, specialized in informing the public on all matters related to anti-Semitism, including war crimes or crimes against humanity.

The murder is indeed becoming an obsession, she said to herself. Victor is right. I must have flipped through this section of the catalogue a thousand times and today for the first time I notice this magazine. She nevertheless printed out the information, on the grounds that one never knew!

Somewhat reluctantly Sara finally abandoned the air-conditioned building, returning by metro this time to her own office at home. In the Lionel Groulx station, a group of children boarded the same train, jostling each other and joking as they passed her. They or their families had obviously started out in a variety of countries and continents, including Quebec, of course. One of the girls wore a hijab, regrettably from Sara's point of view, although it didn't seem to prevent her from joining in the group's activities. Another wore a sari, and three of the boys looked like younger Rastafarians. They formed quite a contrast with the two Scandinavian-type blondes, a boy and a girl, who appeared to be twins. She was amused and pleased to note that, visible differences aside, they all spoke French with the same local accent. Integration was well on the way to changing forever the face of Quebec, fondly and commonly referred to as "la belle province."

Once home, Sara regretted yet again that the ceiling fan was not always sufficient to create a pleasantly cool atmosphere. Needs must, however, but she decided before settling down to a few hours' work, to open a file on "her" murder. She proceeded to feed all the information she possessed and all her hypotheses into the computer, wishing she knew more about cross-indexing and other such short cuts. The task was so absorbing, and time-consuming as well, that she was suddenly startled, on hearing a key in the front door, to realize that Victor was home and the whole afternoon had gone past. Hastily closing her document, she went downstairs to greet him.

"What, not ready!" he exclaimed. "I was looking forward to a long cool shower but I can see that with two of us to use the bathroom it's going to be the usual sprint. Of course, I could go downstairs."

"Shower? Ready? Am I missing something?" Sara was clearly confused.

"Look at your calendar. Cocktails chez Henri. Celebrating Zohra's new book. Among other things. Actually, it's probably just an excuse for a party. Someone at the office said parties are coming back into fashion. Anyway, they're expecting us fairly soon, so hurry up and take your shower, then I can steam up the bathroom. And foreseeing that you might not yet be quite focused, I dashed out at lunch time and picked up a book of Doisneau photographs that was on sale. So we'll not be arriving empty-handed."

An hour or so later, showered and changed, into the same black dress she had worn in Paris to have dinner with Hélène and Éric, although perhaps still not completely focused, Sara found herself, drink in hand, circambulating a huge and very elegant high-ceilinged room. It was absolutely full of bodies, most of whom were both complete strangers and men mainly engaged in deep conversation with each other, although one could notice the odd appreciative glance levelled at the younger and therefore more attractive of the women attendees. Happily, she recognized enough people to feel comfortable and was able to catch up on their news and they with hers.

Municipal elections and Zohra's latest book dominated the conversation at first. Municipal elections were unfortunately rather boring as a topic of conversation, if not devoid of interest for the taxpayer. Montrealers, those who bothered, that is, tended to vote massively for one party for years, then swing equally massively to another, so that there rarely seemed to be a functioning opposition at City Hall. One could get dizzy watching the swing of the pendulum though.

As for Zohra, originally from Tunisia, she had been living in Montreal for quite a few years. In her first novels, she had written mainly about her country of origin, as if spiritually she, or her characters, to be more precise, hadn't quite crossed the Atlantic. The effect was interesting, partly because she was symptomatic of an increasingly significant phenomenon; recently the smells, sights and sounds of very different cultures had been invading Quebec literature, as more and more immigrants or children of immigrants enlarged the body of writers, in French and in English. A far cry from the traditional view, although there had probably always been more writers of foreign extraction than had been readily recognized.

In any case, more and more, again like many of her counterparts, Zohra was venturing into Canadian subject matter, bringing a fresh eye to her adopted country. Although sympathetic, Sara sometimes found it rather depressing. Page after page filled with snow and ice, to be read not just literally but also as a metaphor for the welcome the author or her characters had or had not received. According to the early critics, however, this latest novel promised to be more lively than its predecessors, and Sara was glad she'd brought a copy to get it autographed.

It was obviously popular, or had benefited from good advertising, because Zohra, whose striking Berber face was well served by the flowing ochre dress she wore, was surrounded by a number of people, all holding out both book and pen. Sara decided to wait until the crowd diminished before making her own foray, contenting herself in the meantime with loading up a plate with a large assortment of the excellent goodies on the buffet table. Finally, her stomach full and plate empty, she made her way to Zohra's side, fishing out of her voluminous purse two books, their gift to the hostess and the one to be autographed. The two women embraced fondly.

As, after a few minutes, she was returning Sara's pen, Zohra beckoned to a man standing nearby and introduced him to Sara. "You should already know each other," she said smilingly, "but Richard tells me that's not the case. He's Huguette's Friend." One could hear the capital letter.

If men can be interested in physical appearance, then so can I, thought Sara as, after an assessing glance at the man shaking hands with her, she decided he was quite a catch. Tall, well-built, intelligent looking, handsome in that faintly sinister manner some women still find attractive so many years after Errol Flynn's death, very up-to-date hairstyle, designer suit, just what the doctor ordered, for Huguette anyway. Her own preference went to something slightly more rumpled, but she could recognize other kinds of appeal when she saw them.

Culpably intent on his appearance, she had clearly missed whatever he'd been saying to her after Zohra's introduction, but he seemed satisfied with her occasional nodding. It was probably just the usual introductory chitchat. Perhaps he didn't expect women to respond, just listen. Sara decided to pull herself together, however, to make up for the lack of interest she had shown at her house when Huguette had discussed him. She discovered he too was a lawyer, although specializing rather in real estate. Trying, not vainly she hoped, to look intelligent, she decided to find out exactly what it is that real estate lawyers do that notaries don't. Apart from making it easier for her to carry on informed discussions with her friend, it might also be useful one day for a translation. God, what hyenas we all are! came the thought.

Richard was all charm and attentiveness to her, telling her how enthusiastic he was at the idea of their becoming neighbours. He explained that he definitely needed more space than was available in his current apartment and discussed with her some of the objects he enjoyed collecting.

The decision to make an offer on the house had been taken rather suddenly, he added, but he thought it was not one they would come to regret. Driving by one day he had noticed the house for sale; Huguette had told him how close it was to where her good friends lived. Having to leave her current address was difficult for her and so, of course, was the idea of once more sharing her life with someone else, so he had thought to make her life easier by at least choosing a friendly environment, Sara and her husband on the one hand, the area itself on the other.

Somewhat taken aback by such unexpected thoughtfulness, Sara listened to him extolling the many virtues, some of them hitherto unsuspected at least by her, of the neighbourhood she thought she knew so well. She thought it might be useful to make a point of remembering them against the day she and Victor put their house up for sale. She even added some of her own, in order to give the impression that her enthusiasm for his soon-to-be purchase matched his own. And it was true that having Huguette around, and therefore, she supposed, Richard, would be very pleasant, and not only because she was afraid of being accused of breaking and entering.

They parted after a while in order to circulate anew, but not before agreeing that all four should dine together soon. Richard expressed a preference for a restaurant rather than an invitation to Sara's and Victor's house, in order, as he explained, not to put too great a strain on their new friendship by involving her in too much preparation. A rain check was in order for that. Very considerate. Almost too good to be true. Lucky Huguette. At least, if he kept it up.

The party was beginning to wind down. The room was starting to look scruffy; empty glasses and, on the terrace just outside the open French windows, sadly full ash-trays were starting to outnumber the guests; the uninterrupted sound of multiple conversations was being replaced by long silences punctuated by an occasional murmur. The ambiance had gone as flat as stale champagne.

Suddenly Victor appeared at her elbow, visibly somewhat mellow, if not quite the worse for wear. Definitely not a good idea for him to get behind the wheel of their car. Sara took him firmly by the arm, led him off to say a rather mumbling goodbye and thank you to Henri and Zohra, then headed for home with Victor snoring lightly in the passenger seat. They seemed to have consumed quite a lot of alcohol since her return to Montreal, what with her welcome home, Huguette's visit and now this party. She resolved to move onto water for the next few days.

Once in the house, of course, Victor revived enough to suggest that party food was no substitute for a meal. He offered to make an omelet and a salad which they could wash down with a small bottle of white wine while waiting for the evening newscast which both liked to watch when they could. Sara hesitated over the wine, but not for long, putting off her new resolution like so many others to the morrow. After eating, they sat in a companionable silence until it was time to turn the television on. She debated whether to tell her husband about her own and her daughters' activities. After all, short of a miracle, Peter at least was bound to mention something when he and his wife came to dinner that weekend. Still, sufficient unto the day, she mused and turned her attention to the news.

There was lots of television coverage of on-going crises, including shots in a variety of countries on a variety of continents, of a variety of dead bodies, alone or in groups, all the shots accompanied by indecent close-ups of survivors, grieving parents, children, friends, whatever avid cameramen could dig up, plus pious remarks by representatives of national or international agencies, none of which seemed to do anything constructive. It wasn't news, Sara thought, it was a mixture of voyeurism and navel-gazing.

All that was even followed by a distasteful close-up of the shattered remains of a dead body in Montreal, a man, apparently, who had died of an explosion in a downtown parking lot. The police conjectured that it resulted from gang warfare, although the choice of area was unusual. Sara and Victor looked at each other, shrugged their shoulders, turned off their set and went to bed.

CHAPTER NINE

The Information Highway

Sara sat up in bed with a start, looking wildly around her in the darkness at the eerie shapes whose contours she could only guess at. Slowly she came to understand where she was and struggled to piece together what had disturbed her sleep. The final image was of the face of the *commissaire* smiling invitingly at her from a screen, like something from an insane rerun of the Red Dwarf...

Of course, she thought. Her unconscious mind was making connections that stress made her incapable of during the waking hours. She must find out what was happening in Paris; then her daughters might not need to become more involved. It would be easy enough, surely, to get information on the progress of the enquiry. One of her senior civil servant friends must know someone who knew someone and so on. They were all, after all, *énarques*, graduates of that highly exclusive French school for administrators, *l'École nationale d'administration*. Everybody knew that they remained forever a closely-knit group, moving from the top level at one ministry to the top level at another but always knowing what the others were doing. Putting that in hand would be her main task for the next day. Breathing a sigh of satisfaction, she lay down again and, wrapping the sheets around her, fell into her first easy sleep since the murder had been committed.

Up with the noisy birds again if not with the lark, Sara prepared their breakfast, setting it outside on their terrace and as usual exchanging with Victor the minimum amount of chat consistent with decency. Finally he left the house. Feeling somewhat revived after her several cups of strong Irish Breakfast tea, she quickly showered, dressed and booted the computer. She would check out a few new sites, see what updates there were on her Facebook page, and check out the latest literary reviews published in her favourite magazines and newspapers. She would follow that up with a few e-mails to friends.

E-mailing her friends was much better, she had

decided, than attempting to explain over the telephone everything that had happened since she had seen them. A letter was certainly out of the question. Time, to quote Agatha Christie, was of the essence. She scrabbled in her purse to find the two e-mail addresses she had scribbled down somewhere, promising herself at the same time she would immediately transfer them to her growing list on the computer itself.

Success. She found the piece of paper she was looking for. But, as is too often the case with web-based e-mail programmes, her password was out-of-date. That meant inventing another she wouldn't easily forget. For a moment she panicked, afraid she'd never think of something no one else had heard of. Suddenly she decided to use the initial letters of the first line of a poem by the Welsh-cum-French poet she liked so much, Heather Dohollau.

Hastily she typed it in twice, then, when it was accepted, moved on to read the messages waiting in her "mailbox." After a month's absence, there were quite a few, too many of them in the junk mail category. Fortunately, before leaving, she had unsubscribed to certain lists at least. Two personal messages brought news of friends in other cities; one of a professional nature reminded her that she had agreed to prepare an article for publication. Nothing truly exciting.

Sara then sent long messages to her friends in Paris, explaining what she wanted and why. They had all shown such interest at the dinner party that she couldn't imagine their refusing to help her, particularly as only some more e-mail or phone calls were involved. They would probably be delighted to play some small part in the whole process. Besides, it must be more exciting than worrying about the flaws in the value added tax system, overhauling Customs regulations and other such bureaucratic inventions.

Pleased with what she considered to be a decisive step towards understanding the murder mystery, Sara made herself worry away at her translation for most of the day. Here and there she stopped in order to stretch her limbs and rest her eyes; at lunchtime, she broke off for a quick salad and some cheese. The translation too was taking shape; a coherent style was emerging from all her adjustments and corrections, one she felt she could carry through to the end. Her previous research at the library was paying off, as did probably the fact that she had let her earlier work just sit for a while, rather like freshly decanted wine.

Only one telephone call came to disturb her concentration. She let Ma Bell's voicemail programme deal with that. Otherwise she might well find herself trying to fend off people selling subscriptions to magazines and newspapers she never read or unwanted insurance on the numerous domestic appliances she and Victor owned, on which the guarantee had long since expired. When she saw the person had left no message, she felt even more justified. It couldn't have been urgent.

The cats were the other distraction. They had obviously decided to forgive her, unless what they were doing was a perverse form of punishment. As she returned to her study after lunch, they stalked in too, tails waving. One, Coaltar because of his colour, settled heavily on her feet, complaining loudly each time she moved in an effort to restore her circulation. The other, Rorschach because of her markings, attracted as usual by the static given off the computer, brushed constantly against the screen when she wasn't strolling across the keyboard and producing her own version of the translation. Maintaining friendly relations while progressing with her work constituted a fine balancing act.

As the afternoon and her inspiration came to a close, she guiltily opened the document in which she had stored all the information she possessed about the murder. If she wanted to refresh her memory, she had to finish before Victor came home or risk his wrath. It did occur to her to wonder whether he might not be right to express concern, not so much for her safety apparently as for the effect on all her family, should anything untoward happen to her. She easily dismissed that thought, however, since there was no real reason why anyone involved in the murder should be aware of her existence let alone imagine what she was up to. She could hardly suspect Huguette or her own husband. The information on the screen did not in any case produce much immediate enlightenment, so Sara decided to close everything down.

As her hand hovered over the mouse, however, the thought entered her mind that there might well be information connected to the murder that she was not including. "What a stupid idea," she said to herself, shrugging her shoulders impatiently. "If you don't know it's connected, how can you include it?" Still, it would be a good idea to keep her mind open. She typed in the words "other links" with a row of question marks, concluded that they looked silly but decided to leave them in anyway. With that she finally shut down her computer.

It came to her that, not only had they hardly eaten a proper meal since her return, she had nothing in the refrigerator to make one with. Since it was time to stock up, she investigated her various food shelves and cupboards before taking off for the nearest supermarket and fruit and veggie store. The inside of her car was boiling because it had been left in the sun. She hastily wound down everything that could be wound down and switched on the little fan she plugged into her cigar lighter. Turning on the motor, and with it some air-conditioning, she took off for the supermarket, developing menus in her head.

For that evening, stuffed tomatoes, topside of veal on a bed of spinach, green salad, and *café liégeois*, she thought. Cold espresso poured over some vanilla ice cream and topped off with a good dose of whipped cream would be a perfect end to the meal. For the next day, celery soup, curried haddock, a little broccoli, plus some pears she would poach in wine. Adding all her staples to that, plus a selection of fruits and vegetables, should carry them through until she decided what to prepare for the dinner with Peter and Hazel. At that point, she also realized she had intended to invite at least one other couple to round out the table and hoped she would remember that long enough to get home and make some phone calls.

She was lucky enough to find a parking space immediately but was then confronted by a dilemma. She could never decide easily whether it was better to buy the fruit and vegetables at the store across the road before or after she had finished at the supermarket. The dilemma always reminded Sara of her two brothers, one of whom put salt on his French fries before adding vinegar, so that the salt wouldn't dry it up, and the other putting the vinegar first because somehow the salt didn't get so wet! She herself didn't use vinegar and so lived a simpler life.

That day she chose to get the fruit and vegetables first and leave them in the trunk of her car. She did it all in rather a rush before making her way back to the supermarket. There she wandered up and down the aisles, stopping at the butcher's counter, scanning the spices, wondering whether they needed bacon, cookies, grape seed oil and so on, but all the while she was summarizing to herself the information she had on her computer screen.

One rabbi-in-training, carrying a plastic bag full of old books and a list of names, had been killed on a bus in Paris, although, and that was an extra complication, the murder need not have been connected to anything French. He was known to have travelled to Israel and to Montreal, where he appeared to have some contact with a Hassidic community somewhere off the island. My goodness, and with Huguette too; she must have said that out loud to judge by the stare she received from a woman pushing her cart down the same aisle. No one had yet explained to her in any clear terms exactly what had brought him to Montreal. She should find out.

The books he'd been carrying were apparently not particularly valuable. They certainly hadn't roused much interest, although no one had mentioned to her the results of the police enquiries in the second-hand booksellers in

Paris. Certainly micro-dots seemed a little off the wall.

The list of names had drawn no particular response from Peter, although that trail would be getting more attention unless she called off Claire and Emma, but was it already too late? Drug trafficking had been raised as a possibility by the nice R.C.M.P. man, but it was hard to put that together with a Hassidic community. No one had mentioned other contacts, unless Victor was included!

Of course, the Hassidic community as a whole need not be implicated in importing drugs; it only took one bad apple, and what better cover could there be if you wanted to distribute heroin than an innocent-looking religious group? Could there be an Iranian connection? Would that explain why the *Sûreté du Québec* had sent an officer of Iranian origin? It seemed a bit unsatisfactory to be always thinking in those terms, but someone had mentioned religious terrorism. Nevertheless the murder was hardly spectacular enough for that to be likely. If in fact some fundamentalist politico-religious group from whatever country was behind it, the chances were they would have announced it, at least to the police, who could, of course, be playing their cards close to the chest. Still, her friends in France would be checking up on that possibility.

Solving a murder in another country was no piece of cake, Sara mused, knocking over some carefully stacked boxes because of her dreaming and failing to impress either the assistant manager, or the man whose cart she inadvertently filled up, with her apologies. She felt quite chastened.

Finally, however, Sara finished all her shopping

without further mishap, managed to find a cash line-up where the cashier did not immediately decide to go off duty, close her till and wave everyone off to another line. She arrived home as Victor got out of his car. They carried everything into the house, distributing it all in the proper place, then Sara settled down to preparing the meal.

"Do you want some help with all that? Is there anything I can do?"

Sara brushed off all Victor's attempts at being her apprentice. "I'll be fine. Why don't you run a bath and take a good long soak. It's so hot, I'll be better off by myself in the kitchen, and you probably need to relax a little."

"What a perfect welcome. I am duly grateful. The only thing missing is you standing on the doorstep wearing a frilly apron and asking me if I've had a hard day at the office."

"Move," said Sara, "or I'll take it all back and you can do the dinner." Victor moved, and Sara started her preparations. When everything was under control and while he was still in the bath, she picked up the phone to call her elder daughter and find out why the promised documents hadn't arrived, but Claire was not yet home, so then she dialed Emma's number.

Sacha, obviously back from his conference, answered first. "How are you, mama-in-law? Good to have you home, and indeed to be home. Of course, I was only at a conference and an academic one, at that, not travelling around the world and getting involved in international crime. Sorry to joke about it. Are you O.K.?"

Listening to him, Sara could just imagine his

appearance, the blond, rather lined face, under the unruly chestnut coloured hair. "What a model son-in-law you are, Sacha. You must have taken lessons. I'm glad you're home too. And yes, I'm fine."

"Well, at least it's all a long way away and you don't have to think about it anymore. Hang on, Sara, here's your baby!"

Emma had clearly not brought him up to date on either her own or her mother's activities, and that would probably explain why she chose to answer the phone from her home office in the basement.

She had little to say to her mother, but that little was interesting. The coast-to-coast credit-card check, that she had been able to carry out thanks to a few well-placed friends, had not turned up any dramatic information, although it was fascinating to see exactly how many credit cards some of them used.

"You know, Mummy, I was really tempted to try to find out what those people were buying on all those cards but you'll be pleased to know that better judgment prevailed!"

"Thank God." Sara's response was heartfelt.

A few of the names, she learned, didn't seem to exist in any Canadian files, and as there was nothing to indicate the list itself was Canadian, then they might simply be people who lived elsewhere. In two cases, several people shared the same name, but so far the background check, whether on them or on most of the others listed, showed they belonged to perfectly reputable people, or at least so it seemed. One was a little strange. The name had suddenly surfaced about ten years earlier although its owner, who lived on the Quebec-Ontario border, was quite elderly and had documents indicating she had immigrated from Latvia while still a young woman.

"Well, she can't be a war criminal."

"Why not, Mummy? You've said often enough that women aren't better than men -- or worse -- because they have ovaries. Aren't you being a bit sexist here?" Emma loved to catch her mother out.

Sara reflected on the reports she had read about atrocities committed by women and agreed she was jumping to an unfounded conclusion, although secretly she would have preferred to be right the first time. It occurred to her as she hung up afterwards that she had never even noticed the unfamiliar name was female.

She could hear Victor making noises in the bedroom so it was too late to call Claire again. Sara did, however, get in touch with the friends she had intended to call about the dinner with Peter and Hazel. A gay couple, Ralph and Hugh, one a journalist, one a teacher, and a husband-and-wife doctor team, Stella and Brian. She was then able to announce to Victor when he actually appeared that there would be a dinner over the weekend to which she had invited six people. That should, she hoped, prevent Peter from going on about her visit or the reasons for it.

"By the way, Victor, what day is it? When I come back from a trip, I lose all sense of time, particularly since I don't have to go to an office or do some other outside work that gives life rhythm. I seem to have been back ages but that can't be true."

"Are we so boring? No, don't answer that. It seems like ages because we've done so much. The police, Huguette, the party and so on, and I don't suppose you just hung about over a hot computer all day long either. You've probably been out and about."

"Yes, I have, I suppose. But you still haven't answered my question. If Peter et al are all coming on Sunday, then I need to know how much time I've got to think about the meal."

"Today is Friday so you've not got lots of time. Make up your menu and your list and we'll go either to Jean Talon market or to Atwater tomorrow morning, or both, if you insist. While you were away, I only went to the local supermarket so I need to replenish my supplies of gherkins and so on. Can't have a home without gherkins."

"You're beginning to sound like Rat in Wind in the Willows. Any minute now and you'll have me lazing about in boats in the river. Not a bad thought, but hardly practical."

"Quite right. But never mind Rat. If I don't get to eat what's on the other end of those smells soon, I shall go crazy or turn into a werewolf. I see, my dutiful wife, that you've even set the table, so let's get on with it."

Dinner passed convivially, Victor pausing occasionally between mouthfuls both to bring Sara up to date on his day at the office and to express his appreciation of the meal. He also asked if she wanted to take in a movie, producing a list of possibles from his side pocket, but the response he met with was not encouraging. Sara was more interested in conserving energy for the weekend, and, although he could have gone alone, he preferred as always to go with her. He reluctantly decided he too would stay at home and stretch his legs out in front of a metaphorical fire.

At one point, as they later sat reading in the living room, it occurred to him to query what had prompted her to invite Peter, Hazel and their other friends to dinner on Sunday, so soon after her return. As he started to speak, Sara suddenly remembered something she had to do in the kitchen and rushed out, and when she came back he had quite naturally forgotten the question.

Before going to bed, they decided they ought to catch up on the news and settled in front of the television set. When they turned it on to the channel they needed, the screen seemed to show the same pictures of the same wars all over again, leaving Sara and Victor with the same sense of impotence they usually had, since it still wasn't clear what they could do about anything except possibly write some letters in the illusion they might be read.

Finally, the local news came on with fascinating information about new building sites and heady declarations by various ministers all anxious to organize public consultations instead of actually doing anything. At the very end, just as Sara headed for the bathroom, unable to stand any more boredom, the announcer stated: "The fragmented body of a man which was found after an explosion yesterday has now been identified as that of a geologist working for a firm in Abitibi. No further information is available at this time nor is it known why he was in Montreal. The police are following a number of leads."

CHAPTER TEN

Atishoo-Atishoo
We All Fall Down

Sara's first reaction was to continue towards the bathroom, but suddenly she swung around and moved back towards Victor. "Abitibi, Abitibi, isn't that the area the local Hassidim moved to, you know, when they suddenly inherited some land?" Victor shrugged his shoulders indifferently and suggested once again that she try to think of some subject to discuss other than Hassidic Jews, Nazis and murders. "What about our lovely grandchildren, he asked. Are they not worthy of some attention?" "Of course" she snapped back, "but you must admit it is somewhat of a coincidence that yet another murder, an extremely violent one, should seem possibly once again to involve the Hassidic community."

"Nothing," retorted Victor impatiently, "certainly

nothing in that announcement in any way links the explosion to the Hassidim. It's only your busybody nature that's suggesting it to your obsessive character!" Somewhat miffed, but not anxious to pursue the discussion, if indeed that was the right word for such a querulous response, Sara turned once again on her heels and seemed to progress towards the bathroom.

In reality, however, she was heading for the downstairs telephone. She hesitated for a moment, wondering which police officer she should call, then decided on Danesh, who seemed a little more open than her colleague to «interference» from outsiders. Danesh, however, was not at that point available, so Sara declined her identity to the person answering and left her a somewhat confused message, suggesting that the various police forces might want to check on the Hassidic community in Abitibi concerning the exploded engineer! She added at the end that she also possessed some other information that could help with the task of solving the crimes, a word she now used in the plural. The listener, sounding very doubtful, promised to pass on the somewhat obscure message to the appropriate person as soon as possible

Feeling unreasonably satisfied with herself, Sara pursued her original intention and ended up in the bathroom where she undertook her toilet for the night, sadly noting on the way that neither her semi-holiday in France nor her expensive creams could totally eliminate her developing wrinkles. But Victor seemed to love her still, wrinkles and all, and she was certainly not seeking to replace him.

She heard him pass as he was going to the guest room in the hope that Sara would finally enjoy a quiet dreamless night, and called out to him a friendly Goodnight. He poked his head around the bathroom door to return her greeting and throw her a kiss. Feeling even more cheerful, Sara went to bed, to snuggle down among the nice still clean sheets, leaving a spot for any cat that wished to join her. She lay there quietly, reflecting on the one hand on the possible relationship between the geologist, if indeed that was his profession, and the religious group; on the other, she gave some thought to the object she had noted and admired, wondering about its provenance. She should, she thought also, mention to Danesh that Huguette's Friend, Richard, had been the person who had been encouraging Huguette very strongly to be the co-purchaser of the empty house just up the street. He had, he said, been visiting it quite often in the last few days. Bizarre! Maybe she did hold, at least in part, the key to the whole problem. But How? And Why?

Finally, she fell into a deep sleep, haunted a little by dreams, one of which staged an exotic dancer of a rather Hollywoodian nature, covered in jewels that Sara, as if hypnotized by the chimæra in her dream, found vaguely recognizable. In another, she and Victor were digging energetically at a hole somewhere in the mountains. Sara recalled thinking at one point in this dream that his back must be a great deal better.

When she totally woke up, she wondered whether Hollywood dancer had not been inspired by a fairly recent visit to a Tamara da Lempicka exhibition rather than something connected to the murder. In her day, Tamara, the famous portrait painter of Polish origin, had been the queen of the Art Deco and jazz period. With a faint touch of cubism and sometimes more than suggestions of nudity, her paintings had overwhelmed Society. She painted the rich beautiful, and the powerful, in sumptuous colours, with sleek lines and other voluptuous attributes. But her day had, of course, also passed. Anyway, Sara concluded that Tamara had not been the link to her Hollywood lady. She must look elsewhere. But she did find it amusing that Victor's activity appeared to be confined to digging, although it seemed to be a little useless in the context.

In spite of the different concerns revealed by these night images, she woke up rather refreshed and turned the radio on to hear the morning news, which covered the ubiquitous wars springing up and spreading like poisonous mushrooms all over the planet. Nothing about the explosion of the day before. Lots of heat warnings though, encouraging the young and the old to stay indoors or visit only air-conditioned buildings.

Sara sighed a little but decided to shower and dress before sharing her breakfast with Victor. Her first business-like gesture of the day, after dressing somewhat slowly, was to check the phone, only to discover that no-one had called her back from any kind of police organization, here or anywhere else. Had they received the message, she wondered. No answer came so she decided finally to join her husband in the shade on the terrace, looking, she hoped, her innocent best.

Victor welcomed her with rather a strained smile, as if he had also known a rather disturbed night; he confirmed that was the case, confiding to Sara that her remark about the engineer and the Hassidic community had concerned him more than he had wished to show on the previous evening, although he was not as convinced as his beloved of the accuracy of her ideas. "That is par for the course, as far as you are concerned, exclaimed Sara, but let us not forget some of the other details. Both Huguette and her new love live in individual splendiferous apartments that anyone would give their eye teeth for. Just after I appear to be witness to or somehow anyway involved in the murder of an aspiring rabbi in Paris, these fabulous apartments are no longer satisfactory. Richard decides that his only ambition in life is to live in a house which, although perfectly pleasant, is nothing out of the ordinary. The house is a few doors away from me. In order to justify his new position, he convinces Huguette that he loves her – and, miraculously, all her friends, whom he has not yet met – and that they must move in together and live in glorious harmony on this street. That allows him to visit the area regularly, even to keep an eye on us, and, eventually, he hopes, to get to know my version of events. Of course, he doesn't really want to move in here so he makes low offers on the house, all the while keeping his fingers crossed."

"And Huguette goes along with all this," mumbles Victor. "Of course", says Sara, "after all he is rich, handsome and charming. In her situation he's a very good catch!"

As so often happened, Victor was somewhat bemused by Sara's thought process; on the other hand, he could see how convincing it might appear to a number of people. She then continued. "I keep saying to the girls that there's something in the back of my mind absolutely haunting me. I just know that I have a little piece of information that would probably settle everything. It's something to do with one of the dreams I had last night."

Victor laughed. "Well, as long as I don't have any real digging to do, as in your dream, you should feel free to dig up the information. Have you, by the way, kept the various police forces up to date with your findings? Think how grateful they would be for such help from a citizen! Anyway, while your brain is working quietly to identify the perfect clue, let's just have the breakfast you got all dressed up for. I haven't started making it yet."

"I think" said Sara, "that my training programme has failed. Not only am I not getting my breakfast in bed in the morning, I appear now not to be getting any breakfast at all. You know, I may be already all dressed up, but I could still go into the living room and lie languorously on the divan, rather like a da Lempicka model, while you prepare and serve a special breakfast!" Victor's faint laughter could be heard as he wandered off to the kitchen.

CHAPTER ELEVEN

It's A Cat's Life

Their Saturday morning did not, unfortunately, continue in the same relaxed manner as it had apparently begun. In spite of all Sara's shopping the previous day, they had run out of milk for their coffee and cereal. One of the cats had chosen that morning to throw up, and, naturally, had made it to the newest and palest carpet just in time. A piece of paper bearing an important phone number which Victor had left on the table was missing.

These were all good reasons for irritation but none of them had seemed to warrant the flare-up and mutual accusations that ensued. After all, they so rarely quarrelled.

A sharp word or two, a pregnant sulky silence, a slammed door, and all was forgotten. Fifteen minutes after they had turned their backs on each other and while running her bath, Sara was still trying to understand. It was almost as if, in spite of their good start, they had both got up that morning on the wrong side of their different beds and were spoiling for a quarrel, looking for the merest excuse to boil over.

She ended up wondering whether she and Victor hadn't been just a little too anxious over the previous few days to behave as if she hadn't been away at all. Or as if, while she was away, they hadn't perhaps become a little too accustomed to being alone, one on each side of the Atlantic. Although she wouldn't necessarily have wanted it to last, she was well aware of how much she had enjoyed the total freedom of movement, the idea of being responsible to no-one but herself. No doubt, Victor had similar feelings.

Not wishing to dwell on that thought, she decided officially to put the quarrel down to the heat and, while treading carefully, to behave as if nothing had happened. When she had combed her hair and put her face on, as she was wont to say, Sara went downstairs all ready to go somewhere nice for an appetizing breakfast, Victor was nowhere to be found, so any attempt at reconciliation would have to wait or just be abandoned

Puzzling slightly over her husband's where-abouts, Sara walked down the garden path to the sidewalk only to notice on raising her head that her cat Rorschach was sitting on the other side of the street. With that faintly scary intuition cats demonstrate on occasion, Rorschach turned the moment her mistress's eyes fell upon her, gave a little yelp of pleasure and started running back across the street. Sara walked out into the road to pick her up, when suddenly a huge blur seemed to be hurtling towards her, blocking out all light.

She never knew how or why she achieved her next movement but had the impression, surely false, that she leapt straight up into the air like a large ball on the rebound. She certainly must have jumped because she fell to the ground. As she did so, the thing continued its onward path, rushing past her, its blast bowling her over, and disappearing into the distance. It all happened both tremendously quickly and somehow, at the same time, in slow motion. She lay there numb.

"Sara, Sara, are you all right. Speak to me."

She could hear the voice and others too, calling for the police, for an ambulance, exclaiming over the event, blaming teenage drivers, calling for sleeping policemen on the road, urging her to speak, not to speak, to tell her version, to keep quiet, to move, not to move. It all seemed to be happening elsewhere, far, far away.

Finally the wail of an approaching ambulance stirred her back to greater consciousness. She looked up to see Victor kneeling on the ground beside her, frantically calling her name and patting her hand. His face brightened with relief when he realized she was reacting, although he still looked extremely worried, all quarrels clearly forgotten. "Don't move. The ambulance is here to take you to the hospital for X-rays. The attendants will put you on a stretcher."

"Where were you? You weren't in the house?" Her voice was only a thread.

"Sorry, sweetheart. I felt guilty so I decided to go as far as the local convenience store to get you some milk, or should I say *dépanneur* like most people in Quebec. Naturally I had to bump into Ken. You know what a motor-mouth he is. Half an hour later I was still trying to make my escape. And when I finally did and was on my way back, I heard rather than saw the commotion, the noise of a car going too fast, and suddenly I saw it was you lying there on the ground. But please don't talk. You must keep calm and not move anything. Right now we have to get you to the hospital."

"Rorschach, where's Rorschach?" she whispered. A cloud crossed Victor's face. He could see the bloodstained black and white furry object sprawled unmoving in the gutter.

"She's badly hurt. And frankly, until I know how you are, I can't deal with that. She'll just have to stay hurt."

"No, no. You can't just leave her. Please ask someone to take her to the vet's. Surely one of the neighbours would do it." Sara's voice seemed to come from a long way away.

Her distress was clearly increasing. Victor realized that, whatever his wife's condition, it would do her no good to worry about the cat. He hailed Serge, one of their neighbours, to explain the circumstances, and the man gently scooped up the cat, fortunately to all appearances inanimate rather than dead, promising to do whatever was necessary.

Reassured, Sara then allowed herself to be scooped up

in much the same manner and was borne off in the ambulance just as a police car drew up beside Victor, and two overweight policemen got out, notebooks to hand. Victor was to recount to her later the scenes that followed, gradually perfecting his narrative as he explained to successive audiences the sequence of events.

In spite of the crowd that had gathered, the same one apparently that always miraculously appears after an accident or other dramatic event, few witnesses were to be found. Under police questioning, the three that had seen what happened, two men and one woman, agreed that Victor had been turning the corner when the events took place and had arrived on the scene once it was all over. They agreed on little else.

A car had suddenly appeared, almost out of nowhere, and with frightening speed had hurtled down the street, almost, said one witness, as if aiming for the victim. The others were less sure of that, although the woman admitted she could think of no reasonable explanation for the suddenness of the car's appearance or its speed. She had definitely not noticed it approaching.

The car was alternatively grey, beige and black. It had Quebec or Ontario license plates. The make and model could not be identified with any certainty, although all of them agreed on two of the digits. The police took down the names and addresses of the three witnesses before releasing them to go about their affairs. They then turned to Victor, who had suggested they go inside to discuss what had happened rather than stand outside in full view of the world. After they introduced themselves, Henri Bélanger and

Roméo Turgeon, he asked them to be brief so that he could go to the hospital and check on his wife.

After expressing sympathy, the two policemen first asked for details about Sara, her full name, age, marital and family status, the whole process agonizingly long. Victor responded impatiently, hardly able to contain his anxiety.

After a few minutes, the one called Bélanger, a man in his forties, with a thick mop of almost Indian-looking hair, raised his head from his notebook and, staring Victor in the eye, said calmly: "This really does not look like your usual hit-and-run, sir. Your wife seems to have stood on the sidewalk for a minute or two before stepping into the road. Although there are a number of parked cars on the street, there are no large trucks that might have hidden her from view. And I imagine she would have glanced up and down the street before stepping out."

Turgeon, probably closer to retirement than his colleague, his hair all salt and pepper, and his face more wrinkled, added: "Even if she was careless, everyone agrees that the car appeared very suddenly and bore down on your wife at a tremendous speed. Deliberately, one might almost say."

"Yes." This from Bélanger. "I think we will, as they say, have to keep our options open."

Victor had gaped at that point, or so he said later to Sara. She rather unfairly appreciated with much glee the sudden image of her husband sitting opposite two policemen with his mouth open as if to catch flies. When asked the standard detective novel question about his wife having any enemies, he had been at first inclined to brush it aside as being too preposterous. He nevertheless had to confront the fact that Sara was of course already involved, however remotely, in a police investigation and might indeed have said or done something to provoke the murderer. It was certainly hard, almost impossible, for him to believe in the reality of such a situation; only the anger he felt at her foolishness, her recklessness, seemed to lend it any credence. He made up his mind to tell the police what he knew, however stupid he might appear.

"Well, normally, we're a very quiet law-abiding couple", he had begun. "I should tell you though that my wife recently witnessed a murder in Paris, and the victim had some kind of connection with Montreal."

It was the turn of the policemen to be surprised. International intrigue apparently didn't come their way very often.

Victor had explained as much as he knew but refrained from adding that, if he knew his Sara, there was probably a great deal more to the story. He ended by rummaging around until he found the name of the R.C.M.P. man who had left a message for his wife the day she returned from France, Staff-Sergeant Bernard. With that the two men seemed satisfied for the moment and with the usual admonishment to their host to keep himself available and a promise to wait until Mrs. Thomas felt better before interviewing her, they left to report in at the station.

When he rang the hospital for news of his wife, Victor was told that her admission had been "processed" -- rather like that dreadful yellow cheese, he thought -- and that she herself was in the X-ray department. He should call again a little later when more information would be available. He wandered around disconsolately, wanting to do something energetic to help but aware that for the moment there was little he could do.

Grasping at straws, he decided to call the three couples due to come to dinner and cancel the invitation. It had taken him a while to find all the numbers, because Sara's address book was in her purse, which was presumably with her in the hospital, and the numbers were unlisted. Finally he got the idea of looking them up on her computerized lists; he would have thought of it earlier if he had been less distraught. Both Ralph/Hugh and Stella/ Brian had their answering machines on, so he was able to leave messages without going immediately into details. Peter, however, answered the telephone himself and was most upset to hear about the accident. Victor was careful not to present it as anything else, at least for the moment.

"Tell Sara we'll be thinking of her. I haven't forgotten what we discussed the other day."

"You've seen her since she came back?" Victor wasn't sure whether he should ask the question.

"Yes, she dropped by my office, so we had lunch together. I expect she forgot to mention it. She was telling me about the murder in Paris. Well, you must be anxious to get to the hospital. Thanks for calling and tell her not to worry. Dinner can wait."

Victor put down the receiver very slowly. So, Sara had been to see Peter. It could only have been to ferret out some information. God knows what else she had been up to.

It came to him that he hadn't even phoned their

daughters to break the news. Emma and Claire would be frantic when they heard. He concluded it would be better to wait until he'd been to the hospital and seen the doctor's report. When the ambulance had picked her up, she had seemed not to be badly injured, and the hospital had sounded quite reassuring. He wouldn't worry them needlessly, at least about the state of her health. They would have to discuss what the police had implied, however.

The phone rang as he walked towards the front door. He hesitated a moment, then answered it, afraid it might be the doctor. Huguette's voice came to him. She was returning Sara's call from the day before. Also Richard was with her and had suggested she fix a date and time for the restaurant dinner they had planned.

The news of Sara's accident appeared to give her a tremendous shock. She repeated the words at the other end of the line as if to convince herself of their truth: "Sara run over, Sara in hospital, Sara run over." At the same time, Richard's voice could be heard in the background asking insistently for details, wanting reassurance about Sara's well-being, suggesting a bedside visit, just as if she'd been an old and valued friend rather than a new acquaintance. Victor was under too much stress to discuss details over the phone and rang off abruptly, merely stating that he would call again when he had more news.

With that, resolving to get out of the house as quickly as possible, he snatched up his car keys and headed for the door. Some ten minutes later, he pulled into the parking lot of the hospital to which his wife had been taken, commenting to himself probably for the hundredth time, as he looked at the cost per hour, how expensive it is to visit the sick. At the reception desk they were able to tell him that his wife was now back in a regular hospital room and that he could indeed visit her. The doctor was in the middle of her rounds so it was likely that Victor would be able to see and speak to her. Realizing he had come empty-handed, Victor stopped long enough to buy a large bouquet of rather sad-looking flowers at the volunteer shop before taking the elevator to Sara's floor.

At the nurses' station, he was told she was resting quietly and that the doctor would be along shortly.

One of the two beds in the over-heated room was empty. Sara was lying on the other, white as the sheets wrapped tightly around her, with an IV attached to her arm. Her eyes were closed but on hearing a noise she opened them and smiled somewhat wearily.

"I'm all right. Truly. The IV is just for shock, I think. They've examined me all over, x-rayed my entire anatomy at least twice and so far they've found nothing. Well, almost nothing."

"You're not just saying that? You're genuinely not injured?"

"I promise you. Lots of bruises, very colourful really and, of course, they will get bigger and brighter for the next few days, plus a huge hæmotoma on my left thigh, but, with some anti-inflammatory drugs, that'll go away. They're all quite amazed that there were no fractures, particularly given what they kept calling my advanced age! It quite made me feel like fracturing them!"

"If everything's so good, why are you still here then?

Are they afraid of complications?"

"No, not at all. It's just a precaution. I swear to you."

"Well, perhaps I could just take you home. Would you like that? It would make me feel more comfortable."

"I think I'm too tired to make a decision about anything. Doctor Kielowska, a very pleasant woman by the way, says she's thinking of keeping me in overnight just to make sure there are no invisible after effects. That's why they put me in a semi-private instead of leaving me in the E.R. And I would just as soon. Apparently the police have been asking questions. I don't know why."

That was the point at which Victor intervened to fill her in on what had happened while she was being borne off to the hospital and after. At first Sara hardly seemed to remember the accident or hit-and-run that was responsible for her present condition. As the discussion continued, she recalled the events more clearly, living again through the image of the hurtling mass that should have killed her. Weakly she held out her hand.

"How silly of me. I must have blanked it all out for a while. Only the examinations seemed to matter and the x-rays and whether I was going to get a cup of tea when it was all over. How could that happen?"

"It was your survival instinct kicking in, I should think. Dealing with one thing at a time and waiting until you felt stronger before worrying about what brought you here. The police seem a little suspicious of the accident theory, so perhaps we too should consider other possibilities, farfetched though they may seem. Can I say I told you so? This is not the right time to shout at you but I am angry at you for risking your life like that. Want to tell me what you've been up to?

Sara's brow creased as she made efforts to remember.

"Nothing much really. Nothing, I think, the other people could have been aware of. I went to see Peter, but he certainly wouldn't bruit it all about, would he? Besides, I only asked him about the names on the list."

"What list?"

"Oh, I didn't tell you, did I? The one Bernard and Danesh showed me. You know I have a photographic memory, so when they left I just wrote down all the names."

"Well, what did Peter say?"

"That they weren't on any list he knew about. But Emma..."

"Emma!" Victor interrupted her rudely. "You brought the girls into this! Are you mad?"

"They insisted on helping," said Sara feebly. "Claire was just going to look over their files at the TV station, and Emma only ran a credit check on them."

"Only ran a credit... Isn't that totally illegal? Are you turning them into criminals?" Victor seemed to be having difficulty breathing.

"I didn't want her to do it, but she can be very stubborn. After all, she's your daughter too. Besides, again how would anyone else know? Anyway, she only found one peculiar thing, a woman who appeared out of nowhere, but we're just sitting on that for the moment."

"Is that all?" His voice was dangerously quiet.

"Well." Sara could feel her energy running out, but she knew it was unfair to hide her activities from him. "I emailed my friends in Paris. You know, the *énarques*. Just to see if they could find out what the French police know. I didn't check this morning to see if there was an answer. I can't think of anything else."

"Good." Victor was grim. "You've done enough. I agree it's hard to see how anyone could have discovered what you've been up to, but you have an enemy out there and you're vulnerable. That's it. You're coming home before the day is out. I'm not leaving you here unattended at night. It would be too easy."

"You're being very melodramatic."

"Melodramatic? I'm not the one lying in a hospital bed with an IV in my arm, trying to figure out who might want to kill me. Emma and Claire, your accomplices, can come and sit with you for an hour or two until this Dr. Kielski as I believe she's called, is willing to let you out. I'll stay until they get here, then I'll go and do some shopping."

"Shopping! I did all the shopping. Oops! What about our dinner party? "

"No dinner party, obviously. I've already cancelled. And remember you forgot the milk and various staples? The bottle I bought must be still lying in the gutter where I dropped it. Incidentally, Peter told me you'd been to see him."

Sara looked a little shamefaced.

"You may well hang your head! Anyway, Huguette phoned, to return your call to her apparently. Richard wanted to arrange a dinner date, but I put them off too for the moment. They can wait."

"Before you go out shopping, can you check on

Rorschach? I know she might be dead already but I need to know. Right now I'm numb, but if that, that ghoul killed my cat, I shall be really angry. An innocent little four-legged creature."

"I will, I will, though innocent isn't the word that would have leapt to my mind to describe that furry monster. Let me call Emma and Claire and arrange for them to come over for a bit."

He picked up the phone, and Sara listened idly to his quite succinct explanations as he spoke to each of their daughters in turn. Clearly he didn't want to tell them the truth over the phone. Clearly also, one of them at least had some other engagement for the evening, because she heard him insisting, while still offering no real explanation, that her mother should be given priority. It was probably curiosity as much as anything else, she thought, which would bring both Emma and Claire to her bedside. Victor certainly sounded mysterious enough.

As he hung up, the doctor bustled in to examine her patient. She had an almost stereotypical Eastern European cast of countenance, high cheekbones, arched eyebrows and a world-weary expression. She radiated warmth and sympathy, however, and, after listening to Victor's story, seemed quite to understand his need to take Sara home where she could be properly looked after. Saying her patient was in a satisfactory condition and that she'd make arrangements for her to be released later that afternoon, the doctor patted Sara's hand and trotted off to the next ward.

"Do you think she deals with attempted murder every day? She didn't turn a hair over your story."

"Well, apart from the ever present possibility that she thinks you're a mythomaniac, Dr. Kielowska must have seen worse in Emergency. Besides, she is originally from Poland, you know, and the history of the region has hardly been peaceful. Perhaps she's the norm and we Canadians are the freaks, expecting life to go by quietly, with ne'er a ripple on the surface."

"Well, you certainly make sure that we don't settle into that rut. My mother warned me that I'd never have a peaceful life with a women like you! Actually, of course, that just made you seem more attractive..."

The two of them burst out laughing just as Emma came in with yet more flowers, obviously relieved to see her mother in good spirits. After speaking to her father, she explained, she had called Claire and they had agreed that Emma would come immediately, leaving her sister time to change her arrangements for the evening. She had left a note for Sacha who had left earlier in the day to pick up all four children from their summer camp.

Emma took a quick look at the chart, noting that there seemed to be little seriously wrong with her mother. She then pointed out to Victor, as she bent over to kiss Sara, that there was little point in bringing flowers unless you put them in water, adding she would first find vases to put the two bouquets in before listening to details of the accident, as she still thought it was.

As she arranged the flowers, trying in vain to make Victor's look a little less fatigued, she unintentionally startled her parents.

"By the way, a man whose voice I didn't recognize

called me just now to find out which hospital my mother was in, but at that point I didn't even know you were in one, so I told him he had a wrong number. He was quite rude. I wonder who it could have been."

Victor and Sara stared at each other in consternation.

CHAPTER TWELVE

The Ravel'd Sleeve

Surprised by the reaction to her casual remark, Emma immediately demanded to know more. Given Sara's manifest fatigue, Victor undertook to explain what had happened that morning. In his concentration on the events, he failed to notice the effect he was having on his daughter. As his story ended, he added rather bitterly that Emma already knew more about her mother's clandestine activities than he did and was therefore in a better position to understand why someone was out to murder her. Emma was reeling.

"How could Mummy be the victim of an attempted murder? I can't believe it. Besides, no-one could have known what we were doing," Emma protested. "It's not as if we put an ad in the papers asking for information. Or hung a banner out of our windows. Or announced it on some community billboard."

"Whatever you did or did not do, someone may think he, or even, after all, why be sexist, she, has good reason to kill her. This is no time for justifications; we have to protect her."

Emma appeared almost unable to think about Sara, the shock she must have suffered, the hurt she must be feeling. She was apparently still too busy trying to come to grips with her father's news. She could cope with the thought of an accident, however stupid that might be, but a deliberate attempt to kill? What had been almost a game, although a very serious one, had suddenly acquired an ominous reality, touching her immediate family. Emma realized all at once, as she explained to her parents, how the rabbi's family must be feeling, all the sorrow and bewilderment they must be going through. She shivered in the overheated room. Seeing that, Sara patted the bed-covers, encouraging her younger daughter to sit down beside her.

Victor no longer wanted to leave, but, as Emma quite reasonably pointed out, Claire was also arriving soon. It seemed unlikely that any putative murderer would try to penetrate the hospital in the middle of the afternoon and, on seeing Sara so well surrounded, attempt to bump them all off. Not quite convinced but wanting to get his wife home as soon as possible, he finally and very reluctantly left the room. A few seconds later, he poked his head back round the doorjamb to instruct Emma that she should shut the door behind him, hook a chair under the handle and only open it to her sister and regular nurses. Just as she was about to point out that hospital doors didn't lend themselves to such treatment, a light cheerful voice was heard in the corridor.

"Daddy, what on earth are you doing? Are you coming or going? And what's this mysterious accident? You're not keeping secrets, I hope!"

Claire, laden down with chocolates, fruit and several garish paperbacks, and obviously not caring whether people in the other rooms could hear everything she said or not, came sailing past her father into her mother's room. Once there, she took the fruit over to the wash-basin to rinse it and carefully arranged all the other gifts in two piles on the tiny bedside table, indicating as she went that she hoped he had a really good reason for asking her to cancel her dinner engagement. She spoiled the effect somewhat by adding that David's sister was in any case going to stay as planned with her niece and nephew when Sacha brought them home.

Victor, smiling in spite of himself, told her in a minatory tone of voice to listen carefully to what the others had to say then left the three women to their exchange of explanations. In response to her sister's amazed expression, Emma settled onto the chair beside her mother's bed. Drawing her sister to the other one, she took the narrator's task upon herself, merely glancing occasionally at Sara for confirmation of the details.

Claire was as slow as her sister to understand that their highly respectable, hardworking, occasionally hare-brained mother could actually be the designated target of a killer. Used also to distancing herself from dramatic or tragic events, which she customarily saw only as possible sources of television programmes, she found it hard to think of herself and of her loved ones as being personally involved, to accept that they were no longer mere spectators but actors in a serious drama. This was living news, so to speak.

Emma ended by explaining that their father preferred to take Sara home as soon as possible because he felt she would be better protected there. She informed Claire he'd gone shopping to stock up on various staples, so that he wouldn't have to leave Sara alone in the house in the immediate future. Casually she threw in the news about her strange phone call.

Claire seized on that.

"What an odd thing. You know my phones all flash the name and number of the person calling? It's because of my work. I rarely answer unless I know who's on the other end. There are too many wackos out there; they hear a name on the telly and have nothing better to do than to track you down. You wouldn't believe the garbage we get sometimes. Anyways, as my children will insist on saying, the phone rang a couple of times. Each time it was from a public call box, so I just let it ring. Whoever it was didn't bother to leave any message. Maybe it was the same guy."

"What's worrying about that is that the person must

know not only that she, Mummy I mean, has two daughters but also that we're them. They? It? Whatever."

"You're right there. It's almost as if it were someone that one of us at least is acquainted with. Ugh! This is getting very, very scary."

Sara, feeling more and more like an object abandoned to the Lost and Found, decided to intervene and with difficulty sat up in her bed.

"Hello, girls. This is your mother speaking. In case you hadn't noticed, I'm right here in the room with you. Can we include me in the conversation?"

"Sorry, Mummy, We didn't mean to talk as if you weren't here. Although... there's something to be said for having you in bed and at our mercy rather than the usual arrangement, which is the other way round. Don't you agree Emma?"

Emma's responding smile was a little wan. She said nothing, so Sara jumped in again.

"Let's roll this back here for a while before jumping to too many conclusions. First of all, we have absolutely no proof that Claire's phone calls were anything other than up-front calls from someone who happened to be out shopping or walking the dog rather than at home. If there was no answer, it would be normal to hang up without leaving a message"

"But what about mine?" exclaimed Emma.

"What about yours? It's only if the two are put together that they begin to appear in a sinister light. If Claire's is perfectly straightforward, then why can't yours be a genuine wrong number? People are often rude when they can't get through to the person they want. You know that."

"We both do." This from Claire. "But you're being very Pollyanna-ish all of a sudden, Mummy. You can't believe this is all just coincidence, can you?"

"Well, I admit it's hard. On the other hand, without the accident, who would think twice about the rest? And although I can remember this large black object leaping out of nowhere at me," she shuddered as she spoke, "that too could be a fluke. Another hit-and-run, of which there are all too many. Why would anyone want to kill me? I honestly don't know anything."

"Come on, Mummy. In all the detective novels and thrillers, there's always a character who knows something he doesn't know he knows, if you see what I mean. Ain't that so, Claire?"

"I wish you were right, Emma." Sara sounded quite wistful. "I wish it were just a detective novel, and that a little old lady with white hair, sitting in a corner by a fire, would knit away at the booties she wants to get ready for her second cousin's third daughter's new baby. Then something would remind her of the local butcher or chemist and, as a result, she would suddenly produce a solution, much to the annoyance of whatever chief inspector thought he was the one supposed to solve the murder. I prefer my mysteries in books."

Claire and Emma both giggled, rather nervously though, and Emma picked up the discussion where it had left off.

"You see, Mummy. There may already have been several murders in this case. There has definitely been one murder that we know about, that we know for a fact to be a true murder. So it's no good pretending we're making the whole thing up. It's asking too much to think that everything, the phone calls, the so-called accident, the murder in Paris are just so many coincidences. There's at least one too many in there."

"She's right, Mummy. You just don't want to believe someone's out to murder you."

Sara burst out laughing. "You're making me sound totally unreasonable. Why on earth would I want to believe someone's gunning for me? I'm absolutely terrified at the thought; the more I think about that car the more terrified I get. Of course I'm trying to find some other explanation. Do you think it's fun to know you're being stalked?" She fell back on her pillow as her laughter faded away.

Claire and Emma uttered little cries of concern, bending over Sara, encouraging her to close her eyes and rest for a while. Feeling drained, she did just that, as her daughters settled in, each with one of the books Claire had brought, to maintain their vigil. Emma glanced anxiously at the door, remembering her father's admonishments, and decided to move closer to it so that anyone attempting to come in would in fact be unable to open it more than a few inches. Claire looked startled but, once she understood, kept her peace.

Sometime later, the door banged against the chair, startling all the occupants of the room. Emma jumped up in a flurry, followed more slowly by Claire. They both made ready to block the entrance, but a starched hat and an angry face appeared around the door. They belonged to the duty nurse who wanted to get on with her rounds without any more nonsense. She could not at all understand why two young women first prevented her from going straight in then vetted her credentials before she was allowed to take care of her patient. Nor was she at all convinced by the explanation that Mrs. Thomas was feeling very nervous after her accident.

"If that's the case, then she probably shouldn't be going home tonight. She needs to stay in so that we can keep an eye on possible complications."

Claire cast an anguished glance at Emma but the nurse continued. "Of course, the doctor's already signed the papers, so there's nothing I can do. I'm just a nurse. Poor woman. She certainly looks very pale. If she were my mother, I wouldn't take her home. Well, since she's going to be leaving, I'll just remove the IV, check on her pulse and temperature, if you young ladies will leave us alone for a minute. She also has to sign a release form."

With that she pulled the curtain around the bed. Sara smiled up at her, grateful for the reassuring attention, the bustling authority, the hospital routine, all of which restored a feeling of normalcy. After a few minutes, the nurse pulled back the curtain once more, filled out her chart, explained grudgingly that the patient's pulse was normal although her temperature was a little high, and wheeled the IV machine away with her back to the nurses' station before continuing her rounds.

Emma pulled her chair back to the door but just as she was settling in, they heard Victor's voice on the other side, announcing his return.

"Sacha's with me. He read your note, Emma, and immediately dropped your Suzanne and Daniel off with some neighbours."

"What about my two?" asked Claire.

"David's sister apparently has Marguerite and Patrice well in hand. Anyway, Sacha didn't call the hospital because he didn't know whether your mother would be sleeping or not. He phoned the house instead just as I was putting the groceries and things away. He offered to help collect her, if that's the right word, so he's sitting in his car outside the main door waiting for us to appear."

"I could have done that," said Emma.

"Yes, yes, of course you could, and so could Claire," said Victor testily, "but Sacha's here, and the more the merrier, it seems to me. I'll bring in the wheelchair from the corridor so that your mother won't have to walk to the car."

"You're not putting me in a wheelchair! God, how humiliating!"

"Think of your fractures," said Victor. "At your advanced age."

"You are rotten. Just remember that your age is more advanced than mine. Perhaps you're too old and fragile even to push a wheelchair."

"And just perhaps they'll explain one day," said Emma to her sister as they helped Sara dress in the emerald green jogging suit and brown slip-on sandals Victor had chosen from her closet as being the easiest thing for her to pull on. "By the way, can we just leave? Doesn't someone have to sign Mummy out and settle all her bills?"

"Let's hope she hasn't run up many of those. Not that

she's had much time, poor thing. Not enough even to rent a television set. No, it's O.K. On my way back, I stopped in downstairs and signed my life away. The doctor had smoothed the way, told them we're engaged in something very hush-hush and should be allowed to leave quietly and quickly. Heaven knows what the staff thinks. They gave me the doctor's prescription and said your mother had already signed the release, so all she has to do is get to the car. Safely. Emma, you walk in front, Claire and I will look after the rest."

"What happens when we get to the elevator?"

"You'll go in first since you're in front, but first you'll check it out, make sure there's no gun-wielding maniac in there. You know, I never thought I'd be saying things like that. Not in real life anyway. It's like playing in a particularly bad B-movie, although you two are probably too young to know about those."

"I shall leave the flowers for the nurses," Sara interrupted, as if everything was normal. "And the chocolates and fruit Claire brought. But I do want the paperbacks. If I have to spend another day in bed I shall need them."

"Not the chocolates," said Claire, tucking them into the very commodious purse she always carried.

"You're spending at least one day in bed, well away from the window, and with various members of the family as bodyguards," Victor responded, speaking at exactly the same time as Claire. "I just wish we could ask for some police protection too. Alas, with all the cutbacks, they'd probably laugh in our faces even if we could prove there was a deliberate attempt on your life."

Sara allowed herself to be wheeled out of the room, down the corridor, into the elevator. Nothing untoward happened. It was rather a let-down, she thought, after all the drama they had been discussing. But sometimes a dull life is better, and probably longer, than an exciting one.

Once outside, Victor wheeled her down the ramp to where Sacha's car was sitting. After helping her into the back seat, he ordered Emma and Claire to bring their cars round so that they could all drive home together, in a convoy almost. It was clear that, at some level, he was quite enjoying himself, organizing quasi-military maneuvers, just as if he were back in the Army doing his military service.

"Finding his lost youth again," thought Emma with a mixture of tenderness and irony. "Any minute now and he'll expect us to do some square-bashing or present arms!"

Victor knew quite well what his daughter was thinking. But what she thought was less important to him than his wife's well-being and, to his mind, some organization was necessary. Even he felt a little foolish, however, as the three cars progressed along the streets, waiting for each other before turning corners or crossing at the traffic lights.

"If you put your headlights on, people would think this is part of a funeral that got separated and let us pass with no problem," said Sara, who couldn't help feeling rather like a corpse that was being delivered somewhere.

"Absit omen," came the response. "Heaven forfend. We're home now anyway, so there's no more problem."

With that, the three cars rolled to a stop, Sacha turning into the driveway, the other two parking on the miraculously empty spot in front of the house. Claire rushed to open the front door and turn off the alarm so that everyone else could enter without delay. Sara's step wasn't quite as firm as she would have liked but, with her husband's help, she managed to get into the house before collapsing onto the bench in the front hall. Claire locked the door again behind them all.

Sara's eye was caught by the blinking red eye of the telephone, visible in the kitchen.

"Oh good, messages. Someone get those please."

"Can't we wait until you're settled in?"

"I'd rather not. Just let me sit here for a few minutes and catch my breath; that way you can see who's been calling."

Emma picked up the phone in the hallway and punched in her parents' code. After a few seconds, a male voice identified itself as belonging to Roméo Turgeon.

"One of the policemen," hissed Victor, as though Turgeon could hear him at the other end of the line.

The voice continued, promising to call again later and informing the listeners that the police would like to interview Mrs. Thomas soon but were prepared to wait until the next day. Hugh came next, followed by Stella. Each of them had received the message on their respective answering machines and was calling to express sympathy. Stella wanted to know if there was anything she could do to help, and Hugh indicated he would like to visit Sara in hospital if someone would only tell him which one. Emma, Claire and Victor exchanged glances. Sacha merely looked confused at their reaction.

"No, not Hugh," said Sara, "not possible. He's just asking like any friend. I've only spoken to him once since I came back and that was to invite him and Ralph to dinner. They know nothing about Paris and I did nothing to dispel their ignorance. Believe me. I was mainly inviting them so that Peter wouldn't have a chance to tell your papa that I'd been to see him."

Victor looked up sharply, then a resigned expression spread across his face.

The messages continued. Hazel, Peter's wife, came on, asking for reassurance about Sara's health, and finally Huguette's voice could be heard. She sounded really anxious, and ended by saying that she and Richard were very much looking forward to hearing that she was better, up and about, and able to receive visitors.

"You know," said Sara to Claire and Emma, "I think life does imitate art. You were saying in the hospital that I might know something without knowing I know it. Well, I don't know if it's subliminal suggestion, but I have this sudden feeling at the back of my mind that you're right. Only, of course, I still don't know what it is. I can only say it's as if there were an object there, underneath the surface, just waiting to come up for air. Oh my God, if it's true that I know something, then I really do represent a danger for whomever, or is it whoever as subject of the clause to come?? Oh dear I'm losing all my grammar. But it would mean that he must know it. Or she. Oh my God."

CHAPTER THIRTEEN

Still Waters

"You know," said Sara a few hours later, from her bed where she had taken up residence, "I can't help feeling the attack on me, if it was an attack -- and I really don't know that we've established that, you could all be living out a fantasy drama! -- was the result of an impulse. No-one could have decided to park on our street early in the morning and just sit there forever in the hope that at some point I would decide not only to go out but also to cross the road. It doesn't make sense."

Emma had expressed some concern about her children's state of mind. After two weeks' absence, she pointed out, they might think they were entitled to a slightly warmer homecoming than just being abandoned at a neighbour's house. They had scarcely had enough time to drop off their luggage even. Sacha protested that he had treated them and their cousins to the inevitable Golden Arches on the way home, an experience normally refused to them and reserved for just such occasions. He had, however, reluctantly left almost immediately in order to pick them up again and reassure them that their parents were indeed pleased to see them home.

The others had settled down to a very large pot of tea and a pile of ham and cheese sandwiches before tucking Sara in again. They settled into a sort of conference mode around her, bringing in a few extra chairs from her study.

"Yes, and it's not a sure-fire method either," added Victor in a reflective tone of voice. "Who would have thought the driver could miss on a street as narrow as ours, when you consider all the other cars parked on both sides?"

"What are you suggesting?" asked Emma.

"I'm not sure I'm really trying to suggest anything," answered Sara. "Perhaps your father is. He seems quite offended by the murderer's klutziness." Victor's voice could be heard in the background, protesting faintly. "But the more I think about it, the more probable it seems, assuming a murderous intent, that the person behind the wheel was on this street by chance and, seeing me, decided in a split second to improve the shining hour, as it were. Quick thinker."

"No, Mummy," said Claire. "That's not logical either. You're tossing in another coincidence. Let's say that the person was waiting on the street with no particular evil intent, just watching to see what you were doing, where you were going, who you were talking to, all that sort of thing, then, bingo! out you step, and it was too good to miss.

Oops! Too good to pass up might be a better way of putting it."

"A real hit-and-miss approach," laughed Victor.

"Very funny." Sara pretended to be angry. "Yes, that's sounds the most reasonable explanation. It certainly makes me feel slightly better to be the victim of an accidental murder attempt rather than a deliberate one. Heaven knows why."

"Heaven indeed, because the result must be pretty much the same, don't you agree?" Victor bent over to kiss Sara fondly.

"Rorschach," she screamed, causing him to leap back several feet, knocking his chair over in the process. "I asked you to find out how she is. Why haven't you said anything? What are you keeping from me?"

Claire and Emma were in stitches, watching their father try to collect himself.

"Be still, my beating heart," he murmured grimly, then, turning once more to his wife but keeping a safe distance, he added, "We really haven't had a chance to say much. Rorschach's O.K. Serge took her to the vet's. Apparently she has a fractured leg and slight concussion. The fracture's clean, so there should be no difficulty afterwards. When Serge left her there -- she'll be there for a couple of days, by the way -- Rorschach was complaining vociferously. That would indicate to anyone who knows her that she's fine, thank you very much."

"Such a relief," sighed Sara. "Such a relief. You know, I'm not being stupid about the accidental murder. If it was an impulse thing, then we can probably assume there isn't a sniper lurking on a neighbour's rooftop just waiting to blow me away, if that's the right expression." She shut her eyes for a moment, revealing her tiredness.

Her gesture apparently convinced Victor it was time to leave her to an early night because he immediately ushered his daughters out of the room, promising Sara they would all be only a voice away. She saw him point triumphantly to the intercom plugged in beside her bed that he had bought and installed while she was still in the hospital with Claire and Emma.

"It's linked with the kitchen, the living room and the upstairs bathroom. That should cover most contingencies. If you need anything, just say so. No need to shout. So, here are the pills the doctor wants you to take. After that, you should sleep. I've unplugged your phone. We'll be downstairs." And with that, Sara was left to her dreams.

And dream she did. About a world peopled by enormous vampire bats, wheeling and circling above her as she cowered behind a rock in an unidentified desert where she'd been prospecting for oil. At another point, she was deep in a mineshaft, unable to stand properly because of the low ceiling, walking with water up to her calves, carrying a Davy lamp in which somehow a succession of canaries died one after the other. She knew there would be a gas explosion but there was no retreating. The passage closed behind her as she advanced, her feet carrying her forward of their own volition. Later, or so it seemed, she found herself in an aeroplane, surrounded by people willing her to make a parachute jump, edging her remorselessly toward the door that opened onto emptiness, while she tried vainly to explain that her parachute was still in the cockpit where she had left it. She felt herself desperately gripping the fuselage, trying to resist the pressure, losing the struggle inch by inch.

She must have woken up at that point, still shaken by her dream experience. The bed itself looked like a battlefield, sheets and cover knotted and damp from sweat, pillows lying on the floor. After a few minutes, Sara, collecting her wits about her, looked at the clock's luminous dial. She realized it was morning, past her normal wake-up time in fact, and that somehow, in spite of everything, she had slept through the night. That made her feel better. She pulled herself out of bed to go to the bathroom and on her return found a fully dressed, shaved and pommaded Victor confronting her with a breakfast tray.

"Don't imagine for a second you're always going to get this treatment." He was arranging the tray on the little table by the window. "This is a one-off deal not the beginning of a long tradition. If you were a proper wife, you'd be bringing me breakfast in bed!"

"Nonsense. What's the use of being the weaker sex if we have to lug trays about? I think it's about time I started to do a Madame Récamier or a whatshername? Christina Rossetti, was it? You know, get a long dress, tidy up the divan, move it into the living room, and drape myself over it with one hand languidly trailing and the other possibly waving my bottle of laudanum or something like that. The way I described it yesterday"

"I don't think they hand out laudanum so easily any more. Besides, you've got too much work to do. At least, that's what you're always telling me. Can't have it both ways."

"Well, it was worth a try," said Sara smilingly, pouring herself a cup of strong tea and tucking into her toast and jam.

"After all that, how are you this morning? Did you sleep well? Have you taken your pills?"

"One at a time please." She finished chewing and turned to Victor, sitting on her bed. "Actually, I'm fine, thank you. I feel really good. Truly. I had a lot of bad dreams that I'll tell you about later. They really disturbed me when I woke up, but now, thanks to the tea and TLC, that's over, so, apart from a little stiffness, I'm all set."

"All set for what?" Victor's voice had lost its softness.

"Just all set. Pass me those pills, will you. The pink ones. I'll take them with the juice now."

"All set implies more than just being O.K. It suggests you're off somewhere. What do you have in mind? Out with it!"

"Nothing, honestly. But you can't seriously expect me to stay in bed all day. And nobody's going to burst into the house with a machine gun to mow us all down. I don't want to minimize what happened yesterday, after all I'm the victim, but the impromptu theory seems most likely. I shall just have to be very prudent, that's all."

"You don't even know the meaning of the word!" Victor's concern was becoming more and more apparent.

"Of course I do. And I was prudent before. We all were, Emma and Claire as well. So, there has to be an explanation of what happened, one we can work out if we brainstorm together."

"Brainstorm, schmainstorm. I'm beginning to think your brain's in a permanent storm."

"Victor, don't be like that. Of course, you're worried. And of course, I'm scared. But there has to be an explanation, and we must work on that. Anyway, let's not get excited now. I'll finish my breakfast, have a bath to help my muscles relax, then we'll sit on the terrace and have a coffee. We'll be all right there. Where are the girls, by the way?" Sara was always adept at changing the subject.

"Well, Claire stayed the night. To keep me company, she said. David's sister was already minding the wee ones, since he's still bogged down with the show. You remember that Sacha picked them all up yesterday. Fortunately, the sister agreed to stay over. Claire's gone home now to shower and change and will check back later. Emma's on her way over here now, having gone home to Sacha and the family yesterday evening. There really didn't seem any point to keeping a full house. But I was glad of Claire's company, I must admit."

"And what did you talk about? How to keep me chained up in the basement, since we haven't got an attic?"

"Believe it or not, we managed to find subjects of conversation that didn't include you! *Lèse-majesté*, I know, but that's the way the cookie crumbles. Seriously, neither of us was up to a lot of chitchat so we checked through our supply of videos and found Shane. We had a great time."

"You swine! My favourite Western. You watched it without me. What did Claire think of it? She must have seen it before."

"No, it was her first time, and she loved it. Particularly

the fight scenes, I think. You know nowadays it's all karate and high kicks, then it was all boxing and bare fists. I could feel my knuckles splintering with every fresh blow."

"And that last shot is a real tearjerker, the kid calling his name as Alan Ladd rides off alone."

"And as the old Wild West gives way to the new. Another dream down the drain! Oh well, on with the day."

"Well, if you don't mind taking the tray downstairs, I'll get on with my bath." And with that, she slipped on her bathrobe and went off to start the water running. A minute or two later, while waiting for the tub to fill, she heard Victor go downstairs. She immediately made a dash, albeit a slightly ungainly one because of her stiff muscles, for her study where she booted her computer. A few seconds later, she was into the university server and typing in her new password which happily she remembered. Yes, there were messages waiting! Hurriedly she asked to read them.

The first two were disappointing. A chatty greeting from a friend out West that she would normally have been enchanted to receive but that she greeted this time with exasperation and the second, a one-liner reminding her of a deadline that she had indeed completely forgotten. But the third one, she saw immediately, came from Paris. Jackpot or not, it would surely bring some answers to her questions.

First she had to skim through the customary salutations and an ironic comment or two about the lengths to which her friends had had to go to find the information, lengths that included promises of expensive dinners in the very near future. In essence, the body of the message revealed only that the police in Paris were not progressing very far in their enquiry, except for eliminating a certain number of possibilities. "Including microdots and Martians," added her source laconically. Suddenly, Sara remembered her bathwater and slumped back to the bathroom to turn it off. She returned to her study to read on.

Terrorism and drug trafficking had apparently been ruled out to all intents and purposes, as had the likelihood of a crime of passion. It hadn't occurred to Sara in her wildest imaginings even to envisage such a crime. Given the image she carried round of the downy cheeks of the rabbi-to-be, she found the suggestion rather ludicrous. Then she reflected that the vagaries of the human heart probably never took into account the relative youth or religious beliefs and practices of the heart's owner. After all, why have commandments unless there was a problem to start with? Even so, her mind continued to boggle slightly.

She went on to read that, while several other avenues were being explored, the Paris police were concentrating their efforts on the victim's trip to Montreal. Among other things, he had apparently inherited from a recently deceased Canadian uncle a piece of undeveloped land adjacent to the Hassidic settlement. How strange life is, thought Sara, that he of all people should inherit just that piece of land. His visit, the message concluded, was naturally related to the settlement of the estate and some discussion had also taken place about the desirability of his either donating or selling it to the adjoining community.

That arrangement raised a number of interesting possibilities, none of which were developed by her correspondent. Sara was tempted to meditate on them as she quit her programme, rushed back as best she could to the bathroom and plunged her aching body into the warm and scented bubble bath still awaiting her. There, meditation or no meditation, she dozed for a while until the cooling water brought her back to reality and the need to organize her day.

As she soaped herself, she remembered her previous night's conversation with her family and her own remark about some useful -- or dangerous -- information lurking in her brain at the subconscious level. Try as she might, however, she couldn't raise it. She felt her frustration level, and probably her blood pressure, rising, undoing all the relaxation of the tub. With some effort, she resolved to turn her thoughts elsewhere and let her sub- or un-conscious do the remembering for her. Surely at some point, when she was involved in something completely different, a small, urgent voice would speak in her mind and make everything clear. Or so she consoled herself.

Fifteen minutes later, she, Victor and Emma, who had just arrived, were sitting outside in the shade of a large maple tree. They were enjoying their morning cappuccino that Victor excelled in making and nibbling the biscotti Emma had thoughtfully remembered to pick up on the way, detouring to Little Italy for the purpose.

Sara was reminiscing about an earlier Sunday morning, several years previously, when she had been on her way to the same store. The pavements were covered in snow and suddenly, on a side street, just outside a *café* filled with men drinking their morning coffee and playing various games, her car developed a flat tire. When she got out of the car, several of the men had rushed to the windows and door of the *café* to watch her but not one had offered to help, probably on the grounds, she added a little cynically, that she had no business being out on a Sunday morning without her husband and children!

"But there is a goddess," she added. "I changed that wheel all by myself in two minutes flat. I have never done so well, before or since. Of course now, tires seem to be electronically glued on. Then everything went absolutely smoothly. A miracle. You should have seen their faces. And my smug smile too, as I waved at them when I left. I'll bet they were cross!"

For a little while, Emma and Sara swapped similar stories while Victor looked more and more uncomfortable, not sure whether to defend his sex or decry the sexism to which women were subjected. Occasionally he interjected a feeble remark about faulty generalizations, but his wife and daughter were having too good a time to stop immediately. The telephone managed where he failed. Its sudden ringing coincided with the end of one particularly effective story, and Emma peeled off to answer it for her parents.

Sara heard her agreeing to some suggestion made over the phone but was somewhat startled on her daughter's return to learn that the two policemen who'd spoken to Victor the day before were now on their way over to speak to her.

"It's normal, Mummy." This from Emma who saw her mother pale. "Not to worry. First of all, you're the one who got hit. Secondly, they did leave a message saying they wanted to see you today. Remember?"

"Senility hasn't struck yet, my love. I certainly do remember. It's just that all these discussions with various police forces do leave me a little nervous. I'm still praying they haven't all linked hands across the sea, as the saying goes, and discovered that your father knew the man on the Paris bus."

It was her daughter's turn to be surprised. No one had informed her of that development. She turned towards Victor, clearly all set to interrogate him, but just as she was about to ask for details, the doorbell rang. Having answered it and discovered the police already on the doorstep, she decided it would be more prudent to put off any such discussion until a more private and propitious moment.

After the usual exchange of courtesies, during which Henri Bélanger and Roméo Turgeon introduced themselves to both women and expressed proper satisfaction at Sara's progress, Emma retreated to the living room to read the newspapers. Victor went off to make more coffee for their official guests. The two men sat down and explained that they needed her version of events in order to pursue their enquiries and close the file. Sara told them that at first she remembered nothing but that her memory had finally returned under Victor's prompting. She shuddered as she recounted the dark mass leaping at her and admitted having no recollection of her miraculous escape.

"I remember falling," she added. "But how I got up in the air before falling is a mystery to me. Obviously I jumped, but high enough to avoid a car? I know adrenalin can achieve many things, but turning me into a bouncing ball can hardly be one of them."

"Well, jump you did," riposted Bélanger, "although we don't know how high. But you didn't jump straight up even it felt like that. No, you must have twisted somehow, a reflex action, so that you fell to the side. That's what saved you. Although, yesterday afternoon, we did find some skid marks on the pavement, which we measured, naturally. It's just possible that at the last minute the car tried to avoid you and that, between it swerving and your jumping, even not much, your life was saved."

"You mean that the driver wasn't actually trying to kill me?"

A pause followed as Victor arrived with the cappuccino. Bélanger took his gratefully. Turgeon, manifestly not familiar with the beverage, looked at it suspiciously, piled sugar into it as if to mask any untoward taste, and sipped it gingerly. His face muscles relaxed as the hot coffee hit his taste buds.

"Well, ma'am, we didn't say that, although all things are possible," Turgeon spoke between two gulps. "We don't know who was behind the wheel, we don't know whose car it is, and we don't know yet exactly what happened. So our minds are completely open. Your husband told us you were involved in a murder..."

Sara, casting a venomous glance at her beloved husband as he headed off to the kitchen once more, interrupted in some indignation. "Please don't make it sound as if I'm a gangster of some kind. I just happened to be there when the body was discovered."

Turgeon continued as if no one had spoken. "So we think it's possible that an attempt was made on your life.

The witnesses agree with you that the car appeared from nowhere. All I'm saying is that the aggressor, if there is one, may have had second thoughts at the last minute and tried to undo his or her actions. Other explanations are possible and we intend to pursue them."

Bélanger picked up where his colleague left off. "We would like to know whether you remember anything about the car, anything at all that would help us identify it. The license number, the make, the year, any distinguishing marks like a dent or a special fender..."

Sara wanted to explain that, in that respect at least, she closely resembled the typical female stereotype. She could barely tell a Renault 5 from a Rolls Royce let alone discuss the year or the particular model. But as she opened her mouth to speak, to deny all knowledge, an image flashed across her mind.

"Eureka," she cried, considerably startling her table companions. "I'm sure I saw a Ferrari widget on the front. You know, that rampant stallion or whatever it is they use as a symbol. I recognized it, at least I think I did, because years ago when the world was young, a friend of ours had managed to get one somehow and had put it on his little Italian scooter, you remember those things? It looked very funny with the huge Ferrari symbol on the front. A rampant stallion on something that looked more like a pussy cat."

The two policemen appeared confused.

"But I don't think it's a Ferrari. I mean, I really don't know much at all about cars except how to drive one, but it wasn't sleek or foreign or anything. It was just large and dark and rather American looking, if you see what I mean."

"I'd have preferred a Ferrari," said Bélanger who had finally managed to sort out the information. "At least that would be easy to find, there can't be many in Montreal. But a regular car with a Ferrari horse, if that's what it is, that's like looking for a needle in a haystack. Still, I'll put the word out."

After a few more questions and answers, the two policemen left, seeming rather dissatisfied with what they had learned. They nevertheless announced to Victor on their way out that, as a precaution, they would make sure a police car drove by every half-hour. Reunited with her husband and daughter, Sara started to announce triumphantly that she had finally remembered what was buried. She was telling them about the Ferrari stallion and the police reaction when to their surprise she suddenly caught herself.

"That's not it at all. I know I remembered it, of course, and I did tell the police, but that's not it. It's still back there. There's a piece of information still sitting at the back of my mind, and I can't get at it. And until I do, I can't help feeling I'm in danger."

Victor and Emma felt bound to agree.

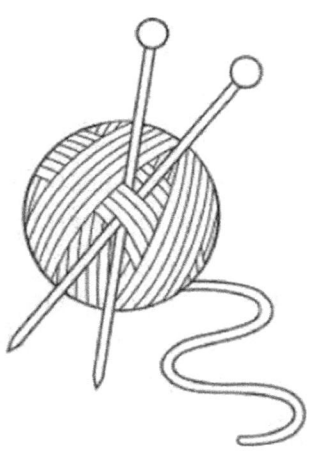

CHAPTER FOURTEEN

Knitting Patterns

"There's an interesting opinion piece in the paper evaluating summer activities in Quebec and talking about the Jazz Festival having pretty well replaced the Saint-Jean-Baptiste parade as the Quebec national holiday, here in Montreal at least." Emma was reporting to her mother about her reading as the two of them prepared lunch, Sara having decided that playing the invalid was too boring. After lighting the barbecue, Victor had turned his creative attention to the tomato plants in the garden.

"You know," Emma continued as she peeled and chopped more fruit for the salad, to which she also added a little fresh mint, "there's a great deal to be said for that argument. Many more people turn out, and they're much more enthusiastic. And, what's more, the Festival genuinely includes everybody. When you're all out on the street listening to music, who cares where you come from or what colour you are? As my friend Nadia says, there are no roots and no branches out there, only trees."

"You're right," returned Sara. "It's too bad I missed it this year. I usually get to a few of the street concerts, the others, as you well know, being a tich expensive to my taste. After all, it's not as if the outdoor players aren't also first class musicians. Edna was telling me, you remember Edna, red hair, translator, husband always wanting to drag her off to Africa, lives in Outremont, anyway, she was saying that more and more events for children are included, so that it's a genuine family affair."

"She's quite right. I was there this year for the big, big night. There were about 200,000 people on the streets, old, young, children, babies in strollers. Amazing. There was no pushing, no shoving, no quarrelling, nothing but pleasantness and listening to great music. There can't be many cities left in the world where you'd get that kind of bonhomous crowd."

"Bonhomous! My goodness. I haven't heard that word for years. Perhaps I can place it in a translation. Too bad it's not the same crowd for the hockey finals; there'd be less looting and pillaging. Our municipal taxes might even go down. Although with the Olympic roof likely to be a permanent albatross around our necks, in spite of all the money it has cost already, who could imagine otherwise, I suppose that's unlikely."

Sara, sitting at the table where she was scraping some radishes for starters, reached out an arm and turned over the chicken pieces that had been marinating in her own special concoction. "Your father should put these on soon. I like my chicken well cooked." She got up to poke her head out the door and call him.

"It's really a slow season for news," Emma added. "Mostly *faits divers* and fluff stories are never terribly interesting. You know, a mugging here, a burglary there. One thing though. Something about a dead mining engineer having been spotted up north." She named a village about an hour away from Montreal in the Laurentians. "Isn't that where that Hassidic community lives that you were telling me about?"

"Yes, it is," said Sara indifferently. "But don't most people go to the Laurentians or the Townships when they visit in the summer? And how did they know what he looked like, if it's the one who was blown up?"

"I expect, once they knew who he was, they found a photo of him and flashed it all over the screen. It was probably in yesterday's paper too, but we missed it. Anyway, I just thought it was a curious coincidence that he should have been seen right there. After all, another murder, another possible link to the players in the earlier one. What do you think, oh *mein papa*?" This to her father who had, as he liked to put it, come running to His Mistress's Voice.

"About what?" he asked, accepting the dish of chicken Sara thrust toward him.

"Emma read that the dead mining engineer they showed on television the other night, the one who was blown up, had been seen near the Hassidic community. His photo's in the paper again today, apparently."

"Really? Well, I suppose it could just be another

coincidence. In what is becoming a long list of them, I should point out. Let me have a quick look. It's not a very good photo, is it? Or at least, not very clear. You know, he looks faintly familiar."

Sara snatched the paper away from him. "I don't want to know. I particularly don't want to know that he's an old crony of yours or a long-lost cousin or anything of the kind. Too much is too much."

"That, my sweet, is what I have been trying to tell you! Be that as it may, as long as you're safe, all this is none of our business. I don't care if he looks familiar, although... No! We pay the police to solve crimes. I don't keep a dog and perform my own bark function, as an American bureaucrat is reported to have once said. Let them get on with it. And I'll get on with lunch. You too." He left to start barbecuing the chicken, obviously irritated by his family's inability to keep the murder or murders at arm's length.

"What about the names, Mummy? Are we going to drop all that? And Claire's videos? Have you seen them?"

"Last things first. Claire hasn't sent her videos over yet. Perhaps she'll bring something later today. I would very much like to view them even if there's no connection to Fainsilber. I don't know about the names, sweetie. Claire hasn't mentioned whether she got a chance to research them. Apparently she has a whole pile of documentation at the office, but she probably can't smuggle it all out. She certainly hasn't had time to go through all the stuff. It was good of you to do your bit but, as you point out, only one is in the least dicey. I'm allergic to witch hunts, so I'd be very unhappy if we brought something on this woman she didn't deserve."

"You always say though that justice must be seen to be done. So why not in her case?"

"Because we're not equipped to deal with it. There are Nazi hunters who know how to sift and weigh evidence. Even journalists know more about that than we do."

"But she could be getting away with murder!"

"She's also entitled to a presumption of innocence. If there's any indication that the crime is linked to neo-Nazi groups, I'll turn the name over to someone, I don't know who. In the meantime, let's just sit on it. She's not going anywhere and time may provide its own solution."

Emma sighed. She would have liked to contribute to the solution of the mystery.

"You know," said Sara, apparently still mind-reading the way she used to when they were children, "at least we can pretty well eliminate the list. That's progress. With what I learned from Paris and from you, we're narrowing the possibilities." She told Emma about the e-mail she had received. Emma was duly fascinated to discover that her mother had been able to dragoon highly placed French civil servants into the hunt, all the more fascinated that she remembered with much fondness her own year as an au pair girl in Paris for Hélène.

"Yes, but you're just making it more and more likely that the engineer was somehow involved." Emma was quite pleased with that conclusion. "I told you his being spotted was important."

"Perhaps so, but we should drop the whole thing for the moment. Let's have a quiet lunch with your father and see what the afternoon brings." With that, Sara pointed to a tray she wanted her daughter to carry outside that was laden with plates, glasses, cutlery, bread, butter, salt, a bowl of radishes, a pitcher of water, a bowl of oriental rice salad. "I really don't feel strong enough to do it myself. You take that and I'll bring the napkins, the fruit salad can wait," she laughed.

"Sure you can manage, Mum? Three whole napkins! We wouldn't want you to strain yourself."

"A mother's life is one long sacrifice," Sara replied, opening the door for Emma and also Coaltar who had suddenly reappeared after apparently hiding out for twenty-four hours. She had certainly not seen him. Probably he was pining for Rorschach. "It's all right. She'll be back tomorrow," Sara bent over to reassure him, realizing only after the words left her mouth that to any observer, and that included Victor and Emma, she must look completely demented. Coaltar gave no sign of having understood her either and stalked off to lie under a peony bush from whence only his tail protruded, like some strange black snake giving an occasional wriggle.

Lunch passed pleasantly, with Victor resolutely talking about general topics, a game Sara and Emma were also pleased to play. Although the radishes were a little past their prime, sharper than Sara liked, the marinated chicken had the slightly piquant taste they all enjoyed, and the rice, with its raisins soaked in lemon juice, mixed with Emma's mayonnaise, was absolutely delicious. The bowl was quickly emptied and wiped clean.

"Ah, there's one we shan't have to wash," said Victor

cheerfully.

Claire arrived in time to share the dessert, and the familiar sisterly bickering began, Emma suggesting Claire do the dishes since she hadn't prepared the meal, her sister pointing out that she hadn't eaten most of it either. Sara was both amused and exasperated. Suddenly she noticed the portentous looks her elder daughter was giving her. Indeed, taking advantage of a temporary absence by Victor who had gone to replenish the supply of drinking water, Claire was gesturing towards the voluminous bag she always carried and mouthing something Sara could not at first understand.

"The tapes, Mummy," hissed Emma. Sara nodded to show she had finally grasped the meaning of the mime.

"There's no point in your whispering, my love," she commented to Emma, "nor," she turned to Claire, "to your continuing with that Marcel Marceau routine. There's no way we'll get to play them without your father knowing. He's going to be watching us like a hawk until this whole affair is settled."

It wasn't clear from her tone whether she was pleased or displeased by this uxorious attention.

Claire nodded.

"I hadn't really thought we'd get away with it but I thought you'd prefer to be the one announcing their existence. That way you get to choose a propitious moment. I haven't had a chance to do the name search, by the way, but, if Emma's done it, would I come up with more than a credit check would reveal?"

"Losing interest?" queried Emma, always happy to catch her elder sister out.

"Not at all. But the tapes and your work are probably enough," snapped Claire. "By the way, Mama, I looked at our files, and there's so much there I couldn't even begin to think of carrying it all over or faxing it to you. The important stuff's on the tapes, I think. We can decide after we've seen them what we want to do next. So, have you decided what might be the right time to watch them?"

"It's an excellent idea to leave it to me, thank you, but the whole concept of any moment being propitious is a little far out. Your papa is going to be very angry, however much we try to prepare him. So, you know me, once more into the fray, I'll tell him now and get it over with."

"Tell me what? I imagine it's me you're talking about? What's the secret? Out with it." Victor waved the water jug over Sara's head in what he hoped was a threatening manner.

"It would be more effective if you had boiling oil," she commented before removing the pitcher from his grasp and signaling to him to sit down. With that she launched into the tale of the videos Claire had borrowed from her TV station and that she had every attention of viewing that afternoon.

To everyone's surprise, Victor grumbled only slightly. Perhaps he was as interested as Sara in seeing the results of the inquiry into the activities and fate of Nazi war-criminals in Canada. Perhaps he thought she was at least safe in the television room, flanked by a husband and two daughters.

Emma, however, announced that she had to leave. The children, Suzanne and Daniel, had apparently not resented her absence the previous evening on their arrival home, but as compensation she had promised to take them to the Old Port that afternoon where there was lots going on to entertain them. A far cry from the days when it was nothing but grain elevators blocking any view of the river.

"Darling sister mine, do you think you could possibly take mine too?" Claire was all smiles now. "David agreed to stay with them this afternoon, but he's feeling very tense with all the work that's left to do. Marguerite and Patrice are bound to get up to mischief, so there'll be an explosion at some point. They were both a bit upset that I didn't sleep at home last night. Perhaps a treat would make it up to them."

"Fine," answered Emma. "Four are actually easier to deal with than two, particularly when two are brother and sister. That way they won't quarrel so much. I'll feed them if you like, and either take them back at bedtime or they can always sleep over. Sacha will be there even if I decide to come back here."

"I think they should be sleeping in their own beds for the first few nights they're back. Two weeks away is a long time for such babies. I'm still not sure we did the right thing in sending them. Thanks anyway but no thanks. I'll pick them up on the way home. On the other hand, it would be great if you'd give them supper. Our kitchen is looking like Old Mother Hubbard's."

"No problem. See you all later then. By the way, Claire, don't take those tapes away when you go. Or, drop them off when you pick up the small people. I really want to see them."

"You're on. I can keep them for two or three days. Try

and get them back to me tomorrow night or the day after. And give all the brats my love."

"Will do. Ciao, everybody."

"Ciao, ciao," the others replied in unison as Emma swung away through the garden door.

In the end, Claire helped her parents to clear the table and stack the dishwasher, volunteering even to make their after lunch coffee, an offer that was gratefully accepted.

"I can't wait," Sara announced. "While you do that, I'll set up the VCR so that we can start rolling once you've served."

"How old-fashioned of you, Mummy. Never mind. Go ahead. I'll bring it all in. You too, Daddy. Just sit down and relax. There's nothing you can do to help."

While Sara fiddled, Victor sank into his favourite armchair, stretched out his legs and readied himself for a long afternoon. Sara then sat beside him in a slipper chair she had inherited from an aged friend who had brought it with her from France and which she always liked to use to watch the small screen. She also armed herself with a pad and pencil in case it should be necessary to jot down some notes. Eventually Claire appeared coffee at the ready.

"I must warn you guys that there's a great deal of very boring footage. This is the totally, and I mean totally, unedited version. So, if Daddy can tear himself away from his little power wand there, I'll do the fast-forwarding today. We can skip over whole chunks and I know which ones they are. Unless you want to be here all night."

She found the loud disclaimers encouraging, grabbed the remote control for the VCR and set the ball rolling.

The opening scenes were all extracts from old footage from the end of the war in Europe that had been taken when various Allied soldiers had arrived at the extermination camps to be confronted by unmentionable horror. Sara, who had seen it all several times before, was relieved at the rapidity with which the scenes whizzed past, although in a way the very speed added to the terrifying effect.

After a while, Claire slowed the tape down.

"This next part shows how well many of the Nazis fared when the war was over. In the Eastern bloc, many of them seemed to have transferred their interrogation skills to the Communist regimes, for example. But the Americans were keen on them too because of their hostility to the U.S.S.R. Here's the bit I really want here."

Familiar scenes from the *Gaspé* flashed onto the screen. Sara grabbed the other remote to turn up the volume, fascinated to discover that a whole colony of Nazis from Germany had settled there in the mid-to-late 40's, forming an alliance with small groups of very right-wing Catholic nationalists.

"I knew that there were French-Canadians during the war who thought we were on the wrong side, all those godless French and imperialist 'blokes', the newspapers from that period are very revealing, but I'd no idea it went that far."

"Well, they're not the only anti-Semites in Canada," answered Victor, "just remember when Jews were pretty well barred from the Laurentians, and that was Anglo, but the Church was never noted for its progressive opinions. Didn't Pius XII refuse to negotiate freedom for European

Jews when he had the opportunity?"

"Yes, but Nazis? Here? The real thing?"

"Never mind that," Claire's voice was impatient. "Let's focus on the video, please. You can have your discussion later or read Alberto Manguel's novel."

As the afternoon wore on, Sara noticed Victor dropping off occasionally only to wake up again with a start, move around a little, before settling again. She too had difficulty paying attention because of the need to speed up and slow down all the time, let alone the effect on her stiff bones of sitting for a long period.

She could quite understand why the footage needed considerable editing, however. Neighbours and co-workers of some suspects were clearly voicing opinions based on malice, jealousy or xenophobia rather than fact. In other cases, suspicions were voiced without much supporting evidence.

It was clear nevertheless that over the years the Canadian government had at the very least been culpably negligent in its screening or lack of screening of potential war criminals. Its recent attempts to bring some to justice seemed to arrive rather too late for absolute credibility.

As the document approached the contemporary period and both the victims and the accused grew older, Sara noted how easy it was to disappear or assume a new identity in Canada. She remembered that no-one had ever asked her to prove she did indeed hold the degree she said she had. Nor had anyone asked for a birth certificate or other proof of identity. She could have called herself Dandelion Jones or Girafe Tremblay or both, and nobody would have batted an eyelid. Such innocence, if it still existed.

When it was all over, Victor heaved a sigh of relief. Claire switched the remote onto rewind. Then all three rose and stretched their legs before silently heading as one to the kitchen and the teapot. Victor got there first and scalded it, Claire started setting out the cups, Sara put the water on to boil.

"That was totally depressing," said Sara finally. "I mean, we all knew about the atrocities, but all those Nazis and other war criminals wandering round free for all those years, here, in the U.S., all over the place. It's dreadful to envisage."

"I like to think they all developed consciences," added Victor, "but would that be enough?" In a gesture completely divorced from the distress on his face, he dropped some teabags into the pot.

Sara shuddered. "It'll take me some time to digest all that. Let's talk about it tomorrow when we've all been able to think about what we've seen. But Claire, what novel were you talking about?"

"Oh, it's something by a man who now lives partly in Toronto, partly in France, but he was, I think, born and raised in Argentina. Anyway, his novel, *News From a Foreign Country Came*, is really quite fantastic. It studies the mind of a torturer and shows the continuity from Nazi Germany, to Algeria, to Argentina and, at the end, to Quebec. Surprised you haven't already read it."

"Have you got a copy?"

"Alas, no, Mummy. I did have, but I lent it to someone who has since lost it or so she says. But you could probably borrow it from the library."

"Well, I wonder if there is a link between the war criminals and the murder."

"Sara, would you please stop?" Victor's voice was almost beseeching. "I know you want to solve the mystery, but do you know how much we care about your safety?"

"Darling, it's too late. If that was no accident yesterday, then the person won't stop. If it was an accident, sitting here at the tea-table and discussing it won't make any difference. Right, Claire?"

"Right, Mummy. But you must be careful."

"I'm being careful. I'm not even thinking about what I know, I mean whatever that nugget is buried in my brain. One thing strikes me though, which ties in with something Emma learned. You don't need a multiple personality disorder in Canada to swap identities; you just change your name. And maybe that's important."

Chapter Fifteen

The Gift Horse

After a light supper, a little *pan bagna* made in the manner of the *Vallée d'Aoste*, that stunningly beautiful region in Northern Italy where *franco-provençal* had once been the official language but where, in spite of laws about bilingualism, that had been somewhat replaced, thanks to Mussolini, by Italian. Sara remembered her surprise on her first visit when she had realized how different their *pan bagna* had been from that of other Mediterranean areas. For the traditional *Valdôtains*, it had involved a pan of very hot olive oil sitting more or less permanently on the stove, together with a pile of various vegetables and fruit, plus anchovies and other like tidbits. At any point during the day, these would be picked up and somehow dipped into the oil until they were cooked to the taste of each person, residents or guests. She would follow this by a tossed salad, some cheese and fruit. A great custom.

Claire had eventually gone home to be with the children whom she picked up at her sister's on the way. When she called her parents later that evening, she explained that Marguerite and Patrice were not at all interested in discussing the camp with her.

"As far as they're concerned," Claire added, "it's now ancient history. The only thing that matters is the super duper time they had with Emma's kids at the Old Port and now they're demanding to be taken there again in the morning. Fat chance!"

Emma had phoned after a Sunday high tea *en famille* to suggest that either she or Sacha come over that evening. From the sound of her voice, however, the afternoon's adventures had taken their toll. In the circumstances, both Victor and Sara suggested she would do better, once the children were in bed, to spend some quiet time with her husband before getting an early night. As they pointed out, they themselves just wanted to sit somewhere in a silent stupor and the police had promised to make regular rounds, so extra surveillance seemed a little superfluous. It was unflatteringly clear that both Emma and Sacha were relieved.

Intent on an evening of reading, Victor and Sara eventually settled into their favourite armchairs, which Coaltar and Rorschach graciously shared with them. While Victor continued to plough his way through a new history of the Napoleonic wars he had started a few weeks earlier, Sara decided that only re-reading the sharp, incisive irony of Jane Austen would bring balm to her fevered spirits.

Alas, even "the truth universally acknowledged, that a single man in possession of a good fortune must be in want of a wife" failed to exert its usual effect and, after only a few pages of her beloved Pride and Prejudice, she found her thoughts turning once more to what she had watched that afternoon.

"Victor?"

He grunted in reply.

"Victor, I need your advice."

A second grunt, albeit more cooperative in tone than the first, issued from behind the tome that hid his face.

"If you thought you knew of a Nazi war criminal, what would you do?"

Victor closed his book, keeping his finger in the page. "Don't you ever give up?" he asked somewhat querulously. "No, no response required, it's a stupid question. I already know the answer. Whatever made me think that one day you'd grow up or grow intelligent! What now?"

"You remember the credit check Emma was responsible for? Don't roll your eyes like that. First of all, you look moronic, and secondly, it turned out to be a good idea. Anyway, she found someone on the list - you haven't forgotten the list - who only seems to have existed for about ten years although she's quite elderly."

"She's lucky. You're certainly not going to make it to elderly if you carry on like this."

"Oh Victor, you're so crabby sometimes. Is this what I have to look forward to in your old age and mine? To continue. This person appears to be Latvian..."

"And that makes her a war criminal?"

"Of course not! But, taken together with what looks like a new identity, you have to wonder. After all, many Latvians must have collaborated with the Nazis during the Occupation."

Victor put his book down on the floor, thereby losing his page. "Let me get this straight. Through some activity either illegal, unethical or both, Emma has dug up a name that you find suspicious because it belongs to someone of a certain age, probably from Latvia, who only started borrowing money recently. Even you must admit that pretty well the only way to get a credit rating is to borrow money and that if you pay cash for everything, you don't exist and you're a credit risk. That's their crazy logic, and maybe, until she retired, this lady always paid cash like a good European of her generation."

"You're reacting basically the way I did when Emma told me. But since seeing that footage today, it seems to me one can't just wash one's hands of the whole thing. It would be like becoming an accomplice."

"You're exaggerating as usual. Oh, I suppose I have to admit, reluctantly mind you, that you've probably got a point there. My preference, God knows, would be to stay a long way away from everything to do with this murder. But, you're right, there is a moral issue involved. Not to mention the fact that you'll give me no peace unless something is done. So, you have my blessing. Call that chap Bernard in the morning. Or his sidekick, the woman from the *Sûreté* you told me about. They're the police. They have ways of checking. If she's innocent, nothing will happen. At least let's hope so. If she isn't, you'll have done humanity a service."

"I knew you'd come round to my way of thinking. That makes me feel a lot better." Sara smiled affectionately at Victor as he resolutely picked up his book once more and flipped through the pages trying to remember where he had left off. "So much so that I can take myself off to bed with a clear conscience. Me and my bruises. When are you coming up?"

"Not for a while. I'll do the guest room routine again anyway. With those bruises you don't need me tossing and turning. I'll put the cat out too, so nothing will disturb you." He reached out to stroke her hand. "Please try to sleep well. The sheets can't take another night like last night, and frankly neither can I. Claire and I both heard you crying out. So much for your pills."

"No, tonight I shall have a proper rest. Not to worry. And just remember the famous motto that Scarlett O'Hara unwittingly bequeathed to all women: tomorrow is another day." Sara's step was almost jaunty as she set off to the bathroom to prepare for the night.

Before settling in himself, Victor set the alarm, a new

practice for them both, since they normally thought of it only when they were leaving the house empty. "*Autres temps, autres mœurs,*" he thought sadly as he armed the house against possible intruders. "Other days, other ways, to quote the Brits". He hoped he would also remember to disarm it again in the morning before going downstairs and setting off the siren to rouse the entire neighbourhood. That would make him even more unpopular than the man over the way who always and noisily mowed his lawn at what appeared to be the crack of dawn on Sundays.

The night passed uneventfully enough, marked only in Sara's case by intermittent dreams of Lucullan feasts where the entertainment was provided by bejewelled dancers who accompanied themselves on the lyre. At some point, one woman danced towards Sara in a sinuous and sensual movement and teasingly shook her dangling, beautifully crafted earrings in her face, nimbly leaping out of reach, however, when Sara stretched out her hand to touch them.

She awoke refreshed, feeling hardly any stiffness in her muscles. The dawn chorus had obviously long come and long gone before she reached consciousness. After some respite on the weekend, the day promised to bring the usual summer heat and humidity. The temperature, according to the radio, was not only already close to 26°C and climbing, but the humidity index was at a very high level indeed. "A day for R&R," she thought.

As she started moving around, Victor's voice could be heard from the kitchen.

"If you're up and about, come and have breakfast on the terrace. Eggs Benedict, How's that?"

"Fine," she called back. "Have you really made my favourite dish? I can see that I've been playing my cards very badly over the years. You could probably have been trained to serve me something every morning. Now I find out."

"Forget it. I'm not trainable. My mother always told me that and I warned you yesterday not to expect too much. So, are you ready?"

"I'm just slipping on something more comfortable, as Mae West probably did not say. Here I come."

And with that, she appeared at the door of the kitchen wearing the frothiest dressing gown she could find. Victor whistled appreciatively.

"But why are you still here?" she asked suddenly. "Isn't this Monday? Don't tell me I don't even know what day it is any more. Shouldn't you be at work?"

"I called in sick. Actually, I just called in, period. None of their business. Besides, I couldn't quite face saying to the receptionist that I was taking the day off to stay with my wife, the attempted murder victim! They'll be O.K. without me and I'll feel safer if I'm here with you. Claire and Emma have their own occupation, as do David and Sacha. No, it's better this way."

"What about all the boyfriends I've invited over for this afternoon?" queried Sara.

"They'll either have to make different arrangements or deal with your husband." Victor unsuccessfully attempted a jealous frown, as he and Sara laughed together.

"Well, I must make a list of things to do. For starters, there's the phone call to Soraya Danesh, at least I think that's her name. That's an absolute priority. The question is, before or after my shower?"

"Such vital decisions can't be taken by a mere man," answered Victor as he cleared the table. "I'm staying out of it. And I might as well get some things done around the house too, since I'm home. Off you go. I'll stack the dishwasher."

Sara went upstairs, deciding as she reached her study that she'd best get her unpleasant duty over with. It took her a few minutes to run to earth the number the policewoman had given her but eventually she found it. The phone was picked up at the other end after a few rings.

Sara stumbled a little as she attempted to explain, glossing as rapidly as possible over Emma's role and laying heavy emphasis on the duty of every citizen to uphold the law. The young woman appeared unconvinced by Sara's protestations.

"Could you just repeat to me how you acquired this information?"

"Well, my daughter was running a credit check..."

"And it just happened that the name of the very person she was checking on was also on the list that was found on the murdered rabbi in Paris? It was all a coincidence? Is that what you're telling me?"

Sara had the grace to blush a little.

"Well, not exactly. But it doesn't really matter, does it, I mean why she was checking?"

"Mrs. Thomas, are you and your family playing some kind of detective game here? Do you think you're in the movies? When we came to see you last week, you seemed a little over eager; during the weekend, we learned you may have been attacked. Now you're calling about a confidential list. I have to express my concern about your activities."

"You're quite right, Ms. Danesh. Can't we just forget all that, though, and concentrate on what's really important. Oh, I don't mean that exactly. Of course, you know what's important. But whether we were right or wrong, we've come up with this information which you may not already have. It may not even be connected to this murder, but it could be connected to a significant number of murders from a long time ago."

"All right. At some point, you'll have to make a statement about all this, but in the meantime I'll note what you're saying and look into it. Please now stay out of this case and remember we're trained and you're not. Not only may you be in danger, you may be hindering the work of the police."

Suitably chastened, Sara provided the requested information, then hung up the phone and decided to get on with her day. After a quick shower, she decided to settle in for an hour or two of translation. The familiar task, she felt, would do much to settle her nerves as well as helping her to meet the looming deadline. With the ceiling fan turning, she turned on her computer, deciding to check her e-mail before turning to her main task.

This time the first message came from her bank asking her to get in touch at her earliest convenience. How irritating, she thought, not to be told why they wanted to speak to her. And speak was probably the wrong word anyway. If she called the bank, she'd probably find herself confronted by what they euphemistically called 'voice mail', punching interminable buttons without ever actually communicating with a real person. Since in any case it was unlikely they'd discovered a million dollar error in her favour, she decided to put off the ordeal until she felt stronger.

The second was from Paris. One of her *énarque* friends informing her that nothing appeared to be moving at their end and wanting to know if Sara had done her Miss Marple yet, solving the problem for the police by comparing the situation to some occurrence in a quiet village in the Townships, where a famous Canadian novelist set her murder mysteries. They were all waiting, the screen said, with bated breath for the next chapter in their friend's story. Sara was very tempted to give details about the accident-cum-murder attempt on her. She finally concluded after her brush with Danesh that discretion was the better part of valor and contented herself with replying that Miss Marple was losing her touch for the moment, not least because she no longer knew of any quiet villages anywhere.

Moving on from her email, Sara checked the weather reports for Quebec, which announced more heat and humidity and what was called a weather watch. From that she inferred they meant the risk of thunderstorms and heavy rain. Fortunately she was staying indoors anyway, since her only obligation outside the house in the next few days was a return visit to the hospital, scheduled for Thursday. She checked her newsfeeds for anything happening in France but found nothing to interest her particularly, even if she sympathized with all those affected by drought in one half of the country and flooding in the other.

As she pulled out her translation which had of necessity been decanting over the weekend, the phone rang and, heedless of her beloved husband's recommendation, she answered it immediately.

"How are you?" came a voice which she recognized as belonging to Huguette. "I wanted to call yesterday or drop by but decided eventually you and Victor probably needed to be left alone for a while. Richard had phoned the hospital Saturday evening and was told you'd gone home. My dear, if you weren't my best friend, I'd be quite jealous of the interest he takes in your welfare. You two really clicked at that party."

"Well, he's certainly very good-looking and there can be no question about his charm," laughed Sara, "but he's not really my type, you know. Not perhaps that in other circumstances I couldn't be persuaded!"

"Leave the circumstances the way they are. Tell me, do you feel up to a visit? I have one or two things to clear up; after that I have nothing special on my plate for a few hours. I could pick something up on the way over and we'll have lunch together. You can tell me how it all happened."

"Great idea. There'll be three of us. Victor didn't go in to work today."

"Really! I didn't expect him to be home. I thought you'd be by yourself, that's why I suggested coming over. What's the matter? Is he ill? Was he in the same accident? What on earth made him stay home? You sound O.K., so you probably don't require nursing. If you've got Victor, perhaps you'd rather I stayed away. We can leave it to another day."

"I'll explain all when you get here," replied Sara mysteriously. "And of course I don't want you to stay away. What a silly question. You must come. What time can we expect you?"

"Well, if you insist. How about noon? I'll swing by the Italian place on *St-Viateur* and bring lots of Italian charcuterie. A couple of loaves of bread as well. Have you got salad makings and cheese or should I get some of that too?"

"Charcuterie and bread sounds good. I'm pretty sure we can find the rest, although this will be no banquet. It's too hot to do much in the way of cooking." As Sara spoke, images from her earlier dream of feasting flashed through her mind. She shook her head as if to rid herself of them. "Perhaps some fruit, if you don't mind. I can invent a lot of things but not that."

Huguette rang off, and Sara went downstairs to break the good news, she hoped, to Victor whom she found in the basement staring at a workbench so covered in tools and screws and nails and plugs and bits and pieces that she could never quite grasp how he achieved any repairs in the house at all. Sometimes she wondered whether that was his refuge against her obsession with putting everything in its place.

He seemed indeed quite pleased at the idea of seeing Huguette again, agreeing to abandon his meditation in front of the altar of home improvements in order to fetch and carry for Sara while she prepared her share of the lunch.

"We had *pan bagna* last night so we can't have that again," she murmured more to herself than to anyone else. "Victor, did you buy cauliflower on Saturday?"

On his responding in the affirmative, Sara decided to make cauliflower salad *à la basquaise*. Once cooked, all it needed really was a grilled and peeled green pepper and a little mayonnaise and that was very simple to make as long as she used extra mustard to make up for the heat.

Later, beating away at the oil for the mayonnaise, she smiled as she remembered the superstition of her parents' generation and before, that mayonnaise made by menstruating women would only curdle. One of her friends had always used that when she was in her teens as an excuse to get out of making it until the day dawned when the mother realized that her daughter menstruated far more than her fair share, almost non-stop, one might say. From that point on Julie found herself making mayonnaise regularly, menstruation or not.

Huguette arrived exactly at twelve, carrying a variety of interesting looking packages. One of the lucky ones, she gave no sign of suffering from the heat, and Sara had always envied her for that.

"I was going to suggest that Richard join us, but he's off somewhere looking at cars. It's probably something to do with his office. He's a car freak, you know, so the big boss put him in charge of the company leasing programme. He gets to decide what they hire and things like that." Huguette sounded quite disappointed. "So, tell me all. You promised."

As they worked their way through the lunch, Sara and Victor brought her up-to-date on events, omitting nothing, and Huguette reacted in the proper manner, expressing surprise, anger, outrage, relief at the right moments.

"What do you expect from this woman Danesh?" she

asked finally.

"Nothing really." Sara was not optimistic. "But it would be neat if she told me what they found out about the Latvian lady."

As Huguette reached across her to pour herself some more coffee, Sara was taken by her earrings.

"What gorgeous earrings," she exclaimed. "Have I seen those before? There's something about them. Where did you get them?"

"Yes, you have," said Huguette. "But you weren't properly awake, I expect. I had them on when I came over last week and you had just got home. Richard gave them to me. Aren't they smashing?"

"You're right. I must have been asleep. Did you tell me where he got them?"

"I may have done. At least, I don't remember exactly, but he brought them back from Europe. He was over there at roughly the same time as you were, although he came back earlier. I know he was in Germany, and perhaps in Italy, but I don't know where else he went. People travel so much all the time, it's hard to remember all the details."

A cold hand gripped Sara's heart.

"So, how did you and Richard spend the weekend?" As she asked the question, her voice came out in a squeak causing Victor to look at her in some concern.

"Not as excitingly as you did," came the reply. "Let me see." Huguette pretended to think very hard. "Yesterday we went up the mountain for a picnic. Then we lazed beside Beaver Lake for a while, doing some people watching, and after that we went to the movies and had supper. See? Very boring really. Particularly the movie, yet another American remake of a French film."

"And Saturday?" Sara's voice had not improved.

"Are you still practicing doing police work?" Huguette sounded amused. "In the morning, I went to the office. Richard, I think, met the real estate agent. Then we spent the afternoon shopping, you should see the new dress I bought on sale, just great. Modesty forbids me to tell you how we spent our evening. O.K. Officer?"

"Is there anything wrong with Richard's own car?"

This time even Huguette noticed that Sara's voice was somewhat strangulated.

"What on earth's the matter with you?" she asked. "Why would you want to know that?"

Suddenly realization dawned and Huguette lost all her composure. Her face first paled then flushed bright red. Her eyes were almost popping out of her head.

"My God! You're accusing him of murder. You, my best friend! You're accusing the man I love of murder! Have you left your senses? How can you do that to me?" Huguette's normally low and pleasant voice was climbing into a screech.

Victor was equally startled. "Sara," he said tentatively.

"Huguette, please don't be like that. Perhaps I can't expect you to understand. I'm not accusing Richard, but there are so many coincidences. Can't we discuss this? He wants the house on this street, he went to Europe and perhaps to Paris, he seems to be doing something about his car..."

She didn't have time to finish her sentence. Huguette

rose from the table, overturning it as she rushed past them to leave the house. In the clatter of falling plates and glass, Sara and Victor heard her cry: "I'll never forgive you, never! I thought you were my friend!"

"Huguette, Huguette!" Sara hurried after her. "Please be careful. Your life might be at stake. Listen to me, please. You know I wouldn't do anything to hurt you. "

Huguette turned round, gave Sara a long basilisk stare and slammed out of the house. The last her friend heard was: "Never again! Never again!

CHAPTER SIXTEEN

Let There Be Light

Sara turned to find Victor standing behind her.

"Did I hear properly? Were you actually accusing Richard of murder?" He sounded most distressed.

"Well, yes and no, I suppose. It's just that I remembered what I'd forgotten. You know what I mean. It's the earrings. That's why I dreamt about them last night on that dancing girl."

"Dancing girl? What are you talking about? What

dancing girl?"

"Oh, never mind. It was just a dream. My subconscious speaking probably. Anyway, Huguette did tell me last week that Richard had brought them back from Europe, but, with the jet lag and all, I hadn't really registered the remark properly. But they reminded me then and they remind me now of a pair I saw in Paris on the *Champs-Élysées*."

"For Heaven's sake, that's about as convincing as your Latvian lady and war crimes. You could probably find the same earrings in every jewellery store in the world!"

"No, no. They're handmade, a one-off deal. It was that kind of jeweller's. Anyway, it's more than that, Victor. I've been uncomfortable with him all week. Why did he absolutely want to move to this street? Why was he so insistent on asking how I was? Who else knew Claire's and Emma's names? I mean, Huguette would have mentioned them. He seemed to know a lot about us."

"So far, all you've proved is that he's an inordinately friendly guy, who takes an interest in his significant other's friends. Sounds reasonable to me."

"But he's in real estate development, and there's that mining engineer. Maybe he knew something about land Richard wanted to buy cheap."

"And maybe they walked on the moon together. Sara, you should be writing novels, not reading them."

"Oh Victor. Maybe I'm all wrong. I certainly hope so. But he'd have a perfect excuse for sitting on this street in his car or just driving along it. Because of the offer they'd made on the house. Don't you see? And now this car freak's off at a car dealer's. Taking off the Ferrari stallion? Exchanging his jalopy for another which can't be identified?"

"All right. Let's suppose you're beginning to make a case here. So what about Huguette?"

"I'm so worried about her. If she goes to him and tells him about my suspicions, maybe he'll attack her next. We should go after her."

"Why? So that we can be attacked too? In any case, Sara, where would we go? Her office? He's not going to murder her there. Her apartment? Why would she go there? His place maybe? But if he's got an unlisted number, we'll never find the address. Let's just call the police."

"I feel so helpless, Victor."

"Of course you do, my love." Victor took Sara in his arms to console her. "You've had more than your fair share of unpleasant experiences. And perhaps that's making you dramatize a bit. No, don't pull away. I don't mean you're making it all up or hallucinating. Just that you're desperate to find a meaning to all that's happened and maybe your conclusion isn't the right one. We'll call the police. They have resources we haven't got."

"You do it this time. You tell them what I'm afraid of." Sara was by now openly crying.

Together they went upstairs to look for the number Sara had left on her desk. The computer screen was blinking at them as Victor stretched out his hand to dial the number. At that very moment, the phone rang. It was Huguette.

"Are you satisfied?" she screamed. "Are you bloody satisfied? Richard's just shot himself." She burst into heavy sobbing, audible even from a distance, and Sara reeled back in shock.

"Where are you? Tell us where you are. We want to help you." Victor used his most reasonable tone.

"Haven't you done enough? I came back here to ask him your stupid questions and he took out a gun and shot himself. Do you hear? He shot himself!"

Victor finally succeeded in extracting from Huguette the address where it had all happened, apparently that of an expensive penthouse condo on a small exclusive street in Outremont. He promised as he hung up to alert the police. They answered his call immediately and agreed to investigate.

The two groups, Sara and Victor, and the police, all arrived at the entrance to the building at the same time. Fortunately neither of the two elegant elevators were occupied so everybody was able to ascend to the penthouse without any delay. Under other circumstances, Sara would have admired the polished brass fittings and leather panels. In her impatience to discover the truth, however, she merely registered Richard's income bracket.

They reached the apartment to find a disfigured Richard lying in his own congealing blood on the floor of the kitchen, the bright red forming a frightening contrast with the stark white not only of the numerous appliances but also of the tiles that lined the walls and floor. Richard had apparently shot himself in the face. Huguette was kneeling beside him, crooning mindlessly, blood on her clothing and hands where she'd clearly attempted to cradle his head. It was a terrifying scene. Sara, her stomach turning over, put her hand to her mouth as though about to retch.

After the first questions, Victor and Sara were allowed

to lead Huguette into another room, a small study overlooking a park, where they used the phone to place an order for hot drinks from the *café* on the ground floor. The only sound for a long time was the dreadful keening coming from Huguette. Eventually she stopped but refused to speak, shaking her head at any attempt by her friends to console her or ask her questions. Only with great difficulty could they finally persuade her to swallow a few sips of the hot chocolate that had been brought up by a very young delivery boy, curious about the police presence in the building.

After what appeared to be an eternity, two officers arrived to question them, the first one, obviously senior to the other introducing himself as Pierre Cartier. The second officer, speaking French with a Haitian accent, identified himself as Étienne Jordan. Both were looking a little harried, fresh corpses were probably not part of their daily fare.

"As I understand what you said, it's a case of suicide," Cartier declared, turning to Huguette. "You were here when it happened, I believe. Why would he wait until you arrived to kill himself? It's a little unusual, to put it mildly. Can you offer an explanation?"

"It's a complicated story." This from Sara who was attempting to protect her friend.

"If Ms. Verdon is to be believed, she was here when it happened and you weren't. Let's have her version first. I'm sure you have all sorts of interesting things to tell us afterwards." The officer was quite firm and Sara, of necessity, yielded.

Huguette then asked if she could speak to the

investigators in private, and they led her off to what was apparently the bedroom. Left alone together, Sara and Victor looked bemusedly at each other, an expression becoming more familiar with every passing day.

Victor was the first to speak. "Well, he certainly wasn't short of money, although it's not going to do him much good, where he's going." He gestured to the antique leather-bound books behind glass doors that obviously belonged to a specialized collection.

"And the knives in that glass case back there!" Sara was pointing through the open door to the barely visible living room. "Look! Trillions of them! All different shapes and sizes. It's an unusual knife that was used to kill the rabbi. Richard could have just used one from his collection. A kvass or something."

"I suspect you mean a kris, Sara. People drink kvass! Well, some people do. "

"Do they really? Ugh! It sounds awful. But you're just being picky. You know what I mean, some exotic knife or other."

"That he just took to Europe with him on the off chance?"

"No, of course not. But he could have found one in Paris that he wanted to add to that lot and just happened to have it on him when he met Fainsilber. He'd probably just bought it at the flea market. Perhaps they met there. What do you think of that?" she asked triumphantly.

"Put like that, it almost sounds convincing. Life must be neater than I thought."

Sara had other preoccupations. "Why can't Huguette

speak in front of us? What's she telling them? Do you think it's the truth? Perhaps it'll all turn out to have been my fault."

"It's natural that she should have a little difficulty facing you and even more explaining about your accusations, although this suicide certainly makes it look as if you were absolutely right. Much as it pains me to admit it."

"You'd have thought Richard would have put a bolder front on it though. Granted there were a lot of coincidences, but you said yourself, Victor, that I indulged in quite a bit of speculation."

"Hush, I hear footsteps. They're returning."

But Huguette did not return. Only the police officers came in, apparently now preferring to interview them all separately. Victor was invited to wait in the little antechamber between the study and the living room. Signalling to Jordan to move away slightly, Cartier led Sara over to the couch where he sat down beside her in the friendliest possible manner.

"And now, over to you, Mrs. Thomas," he smiled.

Sara was quite taken aback, but she launched into the whole story, starting with her appointment with a publisher in Paris and trying as far as possible to stick to the essentials. Her interlocutor's eye glazed over occasionally, but he was obviously making manful efforts to keep up with her narrative, making no interruptions whatsoever. She could only assume that Jordan, who was standing somewhere behind her, was taking copious notes.

At her voice finally tailed off, Cartier seemed to be interested only in the circumstances of the *dénouement*, cutting to the chase, so to speak.

"So, Mrs. Thomas. What it boils down to is that you expressed to your friend, Ms. Verdon, a number of suspicions concerning the deceased. At that point, extremely angry with you, she left your house in order to confront him. Then she phoned you to announce his suicide and to lay a portion of the blame at your feet. Have I got that right?"

Sara agreed that he'd captured the essence although she wouldn't have put it quite like that.

"Well, I don't think I need to keep you or your husband any longer. Just give your name and address to the constable on the way out, will you. We'll certainly need to speak to you again, about this and about all the other things you've told me. I don't have to tell you to keep yourselves available, I expect. You'll know that already. By the way," he added just as she was picking up her purse -- just like Colombo she was to say later --, "was he left-handed?"

Sara thought back to the party at which she'd met him. It seemed so distant, another lifetime.

"I don't think so," she said hesitantly. "I seem to remember him holding his drink in his right hand. And yes, his watch, rather a snazzy job, I admired it; a Piaget perhaps, was on his left wrist. I guess that makes him right-handed, doesn't it?"

"It would certainly look that way," he agreed.

Sara walked towards the door. Suddenly she swung around.

"But...!" she exclaimed.

"Precisely," he agreed again.

Sara wanted to ask a question but was very much deterred by the forbidding look on his face. Huguette was nowhere to be seen when she left the study. Sara wanted to look for her, but Victor took her by the arm, saying only that, as he had given their address and so on already, they could now leave. Huguette was probably giving them more information. Sara looked unhappy but allowed herself to be led off.

When they reached the car, she could stay silent no longer.

"Victor," she started.

"Not now," he said. "For the moment we're going to think of other things. Good things. Our children. Their children. Where we're taking our next holiday. The drink we're going to have once we get home. Please."

On arrival at their house, he maintained his refusal to discuss what had happened. He suggested they both sit outside and have a stronger than usual pre-prandial drink, perhaps a stiff scotch. He escorted his wife to the terrace, skirting the dining room still littered with the debris of Huguette's outburst, went inside to pour the two drinks, and returned after a short while bearing a large tray with both the drinks and a selection of nibbles. He then proceeded to engage in desultory conversation about the grandchildren's development, the weather, the work to be done in the basement.

While carrying on a surface discussion with Victor on these anodyne topics, Sara was left to mull over in her own mind what she had learned. As she absently reacted to his conversation, saying yes or no at what she hoped were the right places, she was trying to put all the pieces together and come up with a clear picture of the events, including the murder of the rabbi-to-be. The sense of this puzzle, in true postmodernist fashion, continued, however, to escape her. There must be a piece missing, she decided, and that was driving her crazy. Or she needed to shift the pieces she had in a different direction.

As six o'clock approached, she decided she could stand it no longer and, rising to her feet, announced her intention of watching the television news. She secretly hoped that world events would distract her from her self-imposed task. Victor at first made as if to stop her but in the end joined her in the television room to watch by her side.

"A well-known Montreal lawyer died in his home this afternoon of gunshot wounds. Police have not yet issued a statement but speculation is rife that this death is related to an earlier killing in the downtown core as well as to a murder committed previously in Paris. Sources close to the victim say he may have committed suicide in order to avoid discovery."

Sara leaped to her feet.

"No, no," she cried, "he was right-handed, I just know it. Huguette put that gun in his left hand because of the mirror image. She's never been able to tell left from right and she's always confused things in the mirror. Oh Victor, tell me it's not true, not Huguette!"

"I can't tell you anything. But if you genuinely believe what you are saying to me, then you must tell the police about his being right-handed and about her problem with mirror images. This business must end." Victor held her tight as he murmured into her hair.

"God damn you. I wish you weren't right so often. But I can't do this over the phone. It must be in person. I'm going to the police station. I know which one to go to. Will you come with me?" Sara was recovering her calm but surely not for long. The dreadful truth about her best friend would hit her before long.

"Oh God, I feel like Judas," she cried.

"Nonsense, at most you're helping to convict a murderer, or murderess, if you prefer. They're not going to arrest her if she's innocent. Not a nice white middle-class lawyer, anyway. The alternative, if you're right, is to let her wander round bumping off anybody who gets in her way. And let's not forget that includes you, my darling." Victor's face bore an extremely grim expression. "Come on, Sara. 'If twere done when 'tis done.' You know the rest."

Sara straightened up.

"Let me just collect my purse and comb my hair, and we'll go," she murmured. "Before I lose all my courage."

A few minutes later, holding on to her husband's arm and feeling for all the world like every copper's nark she'd ever read about, she bravely made her way out the front door to tell her story to the authorities: the house, the car, the earrings, the Hassidim, the land, and everything else she could think of, particularly perhaps Huguette's difficulty with her dyslexia. Soraya was there, as was her original colleague; they greeted Sara quite cordially; they then recorded her statement and Victor's comments very carefully. Finally, after the usual remonstrance about getting involved in police work, they congratulated Sara on her attention to detail and thanked her for coming in to bear witness against her former best friend.

Huguette was taken into custody later that evening.

CHAPTER SEVENTEEN

Epilogue

"I can't believe she would actually try to kill me," Sara said the following evening at a family reunion, after the four young ones had cheerfully gone off to watch a movie she had rented for them.

When the story of Huguette's arrest had broken on the late news the day before, Claire and Emma had started phoning frantically to make sure their mother was all right. Emma was extremely concerned for her safety, Claire laying more emphasis on the impact on Sara of losing her friend in that manner.

Victor had fielded all calls, however, of whatever nature, and allowed nobody to get through, not even his daughters.

"She needs to be alone," he had said to both of them. "She has a lot to come to terms with. I'll tell her you care, that you want to be with her, and she'll appreciate that. It would probably be best if you all came over to dinner tomorrow night, including the wee ones, and we can explain it all then. I think having the grandchildren around will be particularly comforting."

Claire and Emma were on the phone to each other for a long time after that, wondering how best to deal with it. Finally Claire declared they should just go along with Victor's idea. If Emma would take care of the dessert, she would call their father in the morning and arrange the rest of the menu so that neither he nor Sara had too much preparation to worry about.

"Although it would probably be more helpful if she had something to do besides grieving. I mean, I know she's got her translations, but feeding one's family is psychologically more gratifying than staring at a computer," Claire added at the end.

"How true," responded Emma. "Like having a feast after a funeral. Re-affirming life. We'll let her make the main course. A stew of some kind. That's always heartening."

On those rather condescending words, they rang off.

"Well, why did she? I don't understand any of this. Surely she didn't kill the rabbi!" David, like almost everybody else, was looking confused, as he pushed his coffee cup aside to make room for the glass of grappa Victor was offering him as a *pousse-café* after a surprisingly delicious meal.

Claire and David had decided to make tomatoes *à l'antiboise* as openers, in effect replacing the cucumber version that Sara had eaten with such pleasure in Paris, having picked up all the ingredients on the way and using Sara's kitchen space to make the mayonnaise. Sacha's contribution was some Stilton he'd been marinating in port wine for about ten days, and Claire had brought with her a raspberry mousse she'd whipped up during lunch break so that it had time to set nicely in the freezer. Sara, true to form, had, with a little help from Victor, produced a rather good Indian stew, lamb in vinegar and mint, that she served with the obligatory *raita*, that rather scrumptious cucumber and yoghurt accompaniment, and some green beans.

All very satisfying, as naturally were the artefacts offered by the next generation down from among the many unidentifiable objects they had created in their arts and crafts classes at camp. Marguerite and Suzanne had gone in for burnt woodwork, whereas Patrice and Daniel had gone out to collect stones and twigs in order to construct something ecological for their grandparents. Sara lovingly placed all the gifts on the mantelshelf in the living room, wondering how old the little ones would have to be before she could take them off again and consign them to the same cupboard as all the previous efforts made by Claire and Emma.

"And who called Emma about the hospital?" This from Sacha.

"I think I can answer that," said Victor. "Probably Huguette assuming a male voice. If you check with Emma, you'll learn that the call took place before I'd told anybody about the accident. So it was someone who knew not only that it had taken place but also that Emma and Claire exist. And who has their numbers, when one at least is unlisted. Q.E.D. My bet's on Huguette."

"Let's get back to the main story. I'll tell you what I can gather after a long talk with Soraya Danesh this morning," explained Sara in answer to David's questions. "She, incidentally, is the policewoman I saw my first day home. The idea is that Richard probably killed the would-be rabbi. I must tell you also that Huguette apparently confessed to killing Richard, although there's some confusion about her story."

"She actually confessed? What brought that on?" asked Claire.

"Let me tell this my way, Claire, or I shall become even more incoherent. There was some real estate deal involved. The Hassidic community didn't really want to enlarge their territory although they were having discussions with Fainsilber, who may or may not have been in the process of donating it all to them. Richard was hoping to buy Fainsilber's land cheap, but in the meantime, the mining engineer had probably revealed to our would-be rabbi that there's nickel in 'them thar hills.' At least, I think it's nickel. Some kind of mineral at any rate. The police believe Richard already knew that and was hoping to buy the land before its potential became public knowledge, then to lease or sell it to a mining company. That way he'd make a killing. Oops, wrong thing to say."

"It's O.K., Mama-in-law. We know you can't help the odd pun," commented Sacha, while Emma giggled nervously.

"A back-handed compliment, Sacha," said Sara. "To continue my story. Richard was afraid he'd lose out and, in order to protect his deal, apparently killed both Fainsilber and the engineer. I expect he thought killing Fainsilber in Paris would put an end to the whole thing. Apparently, the engineer got suspicious and came tooling back to have a look around."

"But where does Huguette come in?"

"Well, David, when Richard learned that I was the one who'd discovered the body, he wanted to keep an eye on me, so he pretended -- it seems unlikely he was serious after all, he kept on about the low offer he'd made -- to be buying a house on this street."

"Is that Charles and Vera's old place?"

"Yes, that's the one. Stop interrupting, all of you. At some point, Huguette had probably become suspicious. I should add that she was tired of being poor, relatively speaking, and I wouldn't be in the least surprised to discover she was interested in Richard for his money as well as his looks."

"Come on, Mummy, she can't have been that poor." Claire was indignant.

"You have to understand her life. She worked for years for legal aid, she took on all sorts of *pro bono* cases for women who were destitute, you know, divorce, child custody, injunctions against abusive husbands, that kind of thing, and there's no lolly in that. Your services are either free or paid for at a very low rate. She saw all the people she'd studied with, all her generation, most of whom didn't get anywhere near her grades at university, getting seriously rich while her ideals kept her in a very modest income bracket."

"Mum, you're making it sound as if what she did, whatever that was, is justified."

"I'm not condoning anything, Emma. I'm just pointing out that somewhere she's a victim too. The trouble started when she decided it was her turn to be rich, I guess. Anyway, Richard told her what he'd done or she worked it out for herself; after all, she had contacts in the community, so she had to choose between going to the cops or keeping her mouth shut. Given all that tempting money, she not only kept her mouth shut, but decided on top of it to kill me!"

"It really was Huguette who tried to kill you with her car? At first I thought it was a bad joke! You've known her for years!" Claire remained incredulous.

"She told us she was in her office, didn't she, Victor?" Sara turned to him for confirmation. "But we only have her word for that. She may even have driven over here just to visit the house, although it's suspicious that she borrowed his car. Be that as it may, when she saw me crossing the road, she probably grasped the opportunity to get rid of a danger."

"Poor Mummy." Emma was sympathetic.

"Thanks, darling. My only consolation, and it truly does help to make what she intended more bearable, is that she obviously had second thoughts. The police told us there were skid marks on the road where the driver tried to brake."

Sacha chimed in. "So, if she'd had the sense to leave things there, she wouldn't really have been guilty of anything. Perhaps a hit-and-run, that's all. Maybe not even that. No-one hurt and no-one any the wiser. Assuming naturally that she didn't do the engineer in!"

Sara nodded. "Absolutely. Believe me, Sacha, if she'd tried to do the engineer in, she'd have blown herself up. Talk about cack-handed. No, no. Let's work on the principle Richard was indeed responsible for that."

"Where would he have learned to do it?" Victor was curious.

"Oh, I don't know. Aren't men always blowing things up in the country? You know rocks on their farms, fish in the water, things like that." Sara continued over vociferous protests from the three men in the room. "She must have panicked. My guess is that when she went back to Richard's yesterday afternoon and spoke of my suspicions, she realized that if he was arrested, he might tell them the truth about the hit-and-run. She would naturally have confided in him, if only to explain any scratches on the car or to show how much she loved him or something. She couldn't afford to have that information get out, as you can well imagine. On the other hand, he may have panicked too and attacked her. We'll have to see exactly what she says and whether it stands up. Either way, she must have known he had a gun in the drawer. She used it to shoot him, in self-defence or to make her version stick, then she put on her hysterical act to convince us it was suicide."

"And tried to blame you for it," added Victor.

"And tried to blame me. Quite right."

"You know, darling. We only have Huguette's word for all this. She's the one who was desperate for money. She's the one who tried to turn the tables on you. Most of the info we have about Richard comes from her. I'm prepared to grant that he killed the rabbi but I'm equally willing to believe the idea was hers."

"You make her sound like She-Who-Must-Be-Obeyed in the Rider Haggard novel. Every man's fantasy of the powerful evil woman."

"Nonsense, Sara. I'm just pointing out the facts." Victor suddenly brought his hand up to his face in a gesture of sudden realization. "She may not have blown up the engineer but she knew him all right. I knew I'd seen him somewhere. The day I saw her with that poor rabbi in the bus station, she'd been talking to another man, and that man was the engineer."

"That doesn't make her a murderer!" Sara was distraught.

"It's likely to make her minimally an accomplice. You're going to have to face the fact that the more we learn about this case in the weeks to come, the worse it's going to look for Huguette. She probably only confessed to self-defence to try and escape prosecution for the rest. Dead men tell no tales."

"This is a dreadful ending to a dreadful story."

"If I may make a frivolous remark, you should never have noticed those earrings!"

"Well, that proves that Mummy is good at detective work, whether you like it or not. It doesn't feel real, you know, Mummy," added Claire. "Who could believe that would happen to us? to you? I'll never have faith in my friends again."

"We'll all get over it, but losing Huguette like that is a wound that will take a long time to heal." Sara's voice betrayed her sadness.

"And what about the Latvian?" cried Emma, desperate to change the subject. "Was that just nothing?"

"Not at all. That's another story, but with a semi-happy ending," answered Sara. "Although Danesh was cross with us, she told me what they'd found out. No war crimes, no Nazi sympathies. The woman had been happily married for many years but, as he grew older, her husband started becoming violent and took to beating her, very badly, it seems. Danesh says he refused to get any treatment, just did his regular remorse bit, then started again. The woman left him a couple of times but he always found out where the women's shelter was that she was hiding in."

"Probably the fuzz," muttered Claire, who had her own prejudices.

"The point is," continued Sara, "she finally and eventually realized she would have to move far away and start a new life for herself. She got help from some women's groups and, listen carefully, Claire, a community police force. That's why she made a sudden appearance under a new name at her advanced age. A battered wife determined to survive. Just as she'd survived the Nazi occupation, if you like. He died a few months ago so it doesn't matter anymore if the secret is discovered."

"So, all's well that ends well, after all?" asked David

"You forgot something, I think," intervened Victor.

"What?" Sara couldn't imagine what that might be.

"The list. Remember the list?" Victor imitated Sara asking him that very same question a day or two earlier.

"Right," she exclaimed. "How silly of me." She turned to the others. "It appears the list has no connection with Fainsilber at all. At least the police believe it may just be something he found in the book that he bought. It doesn't seem to correspond to anything, so they think it could be any kind of list, you know, a choral society in Germany, people who get to sit at the same table on an international cruise, people you meet on a charter trip to Cuba. There's absolutely nothing to link any of those people together in any organic way, as far as Canada's concerned. The chances are, apparently, that even our Latvian lady isn't the one on the list. It's a common name over there, like Jane Smith or Odette Tremblay. Thousands of women have the same name, and it's just a coincidence that Emma's research turned up something suspicious about one of them over here!"

"You're not serious! That poor woman's got nothing to do with anything?" Emma was outraged.

"I think what I'm really trying to say is that we'll probably never know the truth about those names. So we can call it all coincidence and leave it at that or go even crazier trying to invent plausible explanations."

"Does knowing what you do know though help you deal with... what's happened?" Sacha's voice as well as his words revealed his concern for Sara.

"It helps," smiled Sara, "but all this, you know, having been involved in the Real Thing, is going to make it harder for me to take Lord Littlemore and his perfect butler at all seriously. To think all my involvement started with that idiot translation, which I have yet to do, moreover. And, if it hadn't been for that, maybe Huguette would be sitting with us now."

"She might not have been found out, but if she is guilty, I'm just as happy that she's not here. I'm sorry, Sara, but you'll just have to deal with that. And, of course, with the possibility that nothing will ever be certain."

Victor suddenly struck a pose. "I say, chaps, anyone for drinks? Hey, Lord Littlemore's got nothing on me; I can wave a languid hand with the best of them. Of course, my effete aristocratic accent is a bit off, but what can you expect from us poor colonials?"

Amid general laughter, five outstretched hands holding glasses waited for him to fill them.

"No," said Sara. "You're not having the last word." And with that, she firmly removed the bottle of grappa from his astonished grasp. She disappeared briefly into the kitchen and came back bearing a tray with a bottle of champagne which she proceeded deftly to open and to pour into the tall chilled glasses she had thoughtfully prepared earlier in the day.

"All for one and one for all," she cried.

"All for one and one for all," they dutifully chorused as they in one accord emptied their glasses.

FIN

www.authorwilliams.com

ABOUT THE AUTHOR Gwyneth Williams is the author of this book, although she has traditionally used another name for her various publications: from long academic texts, usually in French, shorter ones for magazines, to funny family stories for children and grandchildren.

Gwyneth Williams is not a pseudonym. It is a combination of her maiden and the third of three forenames imposed on her at birth by her paternal grandfather.

Canada is very open to the idea of multiple nationalities and many Canadians consider themselves citizens of the world. Two passports, three passports, and why not four... Many people live their lives in fairly straight lines while others move in zig zags. Gwyneth's life follows this pattern: born in Wales, lived in England, married in France, ending up first in Toronto, then in Montreal. Her life is divided between French and English, but sadly her Welsh is gone forever.

An avid reader and a great cook, Gwyneth has now finally yielded to her passion for mystery novels and has delivered her own. In this debut novel, she has also brought to life, once again, her Welsh origins.

P.S.

… neither Sara nor her family had any idea of the troubles she had yet to meet!

CPSIA information can be obtained at www.ICGtesting.com
Printed in the USA
LVOW01s2102240315

431861LV00009B/29/P